ANGEL DOLL

It's the dark days of the Great Depression, and former Boston P.D. detective Jack Dunning is starting over after losing both his wife and his job to the bottle. Fresh off the Greyhound, he slips into The Blue Rose Dance Hall — and falls hard for a beautiful dime-a-dance girl, Angel Doll. But then Angel shoots gangster Axel Teague and blows town on the midnight train to Los Angeles . . .

ARLETTE LEES

◆

ANGEL DOLL

Complete and Unabridged

LINFORD
Leicester

First published in Great Britain

First Linford Edition
published 2013

A catalogue record for this book is available
from the British Library.

ISBN 978–1–4448–1762–1

Published by
F. A. Thorpe (Publishing)
Anstey, Leicestershire

Set by Words & Graphics Ltd.
Anstey, Leicestershire
Printed and bound in Great Britain by
T. J. International Ltd., Padstow, Cornwall

This book is printed on acid-free paper

SPECIAL MESSAGE TO READERS

THE ULVERSCROFT FOUNDATION
(registered UK charity number 264873)
was established in 1972 to provide funds for
research, diagnosis and treatment of eye diseases.
Examples of major projects funded by
the Ulverscroft Foundation are:-

- The Children's Eye Unit at Moorfields Eye Hospital, London
- The Ulverscroft Children's Eye Unit at Great Ormond Street Hospital for Sick Children
- Funding research into eye diseases and treatment at the Department of Ophthalmology, University of Leicester
- The Ulverscroft Vision Research Group, Institute of Child Health
- Twin operating theatres at the Western Ophthalmic Hospital, London
- The Chair of Ophthalmology at the Royal Australian College of Ophthalmologists

You can help further the work of the Foundation
by making a donation or leaving a legacy.
Every contribution is gratefully received. If you
would like to help support the Foundation or
require further information, please contact:

THE ULVERSCROFT FOUNDATION
The Green, Bradgate Road, Anstey
Leicester LE7 7FU, England
Tel: (0116) 236 4325

website: www.foundation.ulverscroft.com

1

The Dime-A-Dance Girl

I step off of the Greyhound Bus into the pouring rain. I'm wearing my one good pair of shoes, a decent suit beneath my trench coat and a brown fedora pulled low on my forehead. My leather suitcase carries the sum of my worldly possessions and tucked into my wallet is the paltry remainder of the fifty bucks Aunt Pearl bestowed upon me, provided I seek my fortune elsewhere.

Well, Santa Paulina is about as elsewhere as one can get from the stiff front parlors of Boston. I set my suitcase on the sidewalk and pull up my collar but the rain is already drizzling down my back. If this is an example of sunny California, I wonder what it's like on a bad day.

I head down Cork Street toward the Rexford Hotel where my old war buddy,

Hank Featherstone, is holding a job for me. It won't pay what my cop salary had, but I can drink on the job provided I don't get as soused as I was the day I was allowed to resign from the Force. When I asked Hank what my duties entailed, he simply said, 'keeping the lid on things.' I'm better at that than I am at keeping the cork in the bottle, so I accept the offer.

I'm halfway to my destination when an icy headwind gets the best of me and I duck through the first unlocked door I come to. I find myself standing in The Blue Rose Dance Hall . . . a classy euphemism for a dime-a-dance joint.

Couples are slow-dancing under a revolving mirror ball that throws dizzying arrows of light around the room. In the dark corners, pocket flasks catch the light. Prohibition has lost favor, even among the tight-lipped Bible thumpers that crammed it down our throats, so nobody's all that worried about getting busted. You'd think the building was on fire for all the cigarette smoke. I inhale deeply and cough. Just my kind of place.

I check my things at the counter and

spring for ten dance tickets — like I can afford to blow a buck. I sit on a bench along the wall to dry off and size up the place. Soldiers, laborers, thugs, grifters, and farm boys from the Dust Bowl circle the floor with ladies wearing too much make-up and too many artificial flowers in their hair. Beneath the testosterone and cheap after-shave is the undercurrent of lonely desperation. But hell, it's the Depression. Everybody's on the skids except Al Capone.

I can't take my eyes off the pretty girl in the blue dress. She has a heart-shaped face and a mouth like the pink lipstick kiss on a love letter. The problem is, the jug-eared loser she's dancing with is holding her so tight she can't breathe. She struggles and panics. He laughs and tightens his grip.

I forget about firing up my Lucky and walk over. The guy's drunk. He's not the kind you can reason with so I knock him cold right out of the chute. I'm not the young gladiator I was when I joined the Force, but my fist is still a cinder block. A couple of cheerful young soldiers scrape him off the floor and toss him into the rain.

Now the girl is with me. She looks too young to be out after dark. She's even forgotten the heavy make-up and fake flowers. I ask her if she's okay. She wipes away a frightened tear and nods.

'I'm Jack Dunning,' I say.

'Angel Dahl,' she says, but I take it for Doll, like if she uses her real name some maniac might look her up in the phone book on a dark stormy night like tonight. I hand her a dance ticket and she settles in my arms like a soft little kitten. She tenses and I feel resistance along her spine.

'It's not what you think,' I say. 'It's just my gun.'

She blushes. Her complexion is delicate and pale like a hothouse flower.

'Your gun?' she says.

'I was fifteen years on the Force. You might say it's part of my anatomy.'

'I saw the suitcase. Are you coming or going?'

'I just blew in from Boston. I'll be working security at The Rexford.'

4

'I rent a room at The Rexford. Could we walk together when I get off?'

'Sure,' I say.

The top of her head fits beneath my chin. Her hair smells like roses. We dance slow and sensuous to 'Stormy Weather' and a jazz rendition of the 'Shadow Waltz'. I drown in the scent of her and the knots at my center unravel.

The lights flicker and it's closing time.

We walk toward The Rexford in the pouring rain. I carry my suitcase in one hand, my other arm around Angel. The rain sounds like buckshot on the canopy of her umbrella. Only railroad bums and stray dogs are out on a night like this. Lightning flashes and thunder crackles and snaps like a frayed electrical cable.

We start across the alley between Sal's Pawn Shop and the Rescue Mission when the goddamn Blarney Stone lands in the center of my back. I cave to my knees, nearly paralyzed by the blow. My suitcase skids across the sidewalk. I wasn't paying attention to my surroundings. I was thinking about the girl, how pretty she is, how good she smells, how natural she feels in my arms.

Angel gasps. Her umbrella sails off in the wind. I struggle to my feet, pain radiating from my back into my left leg. Jug-Ears grins and swings a sock filled with billiard balls, a goofy smile on his face. His breath is eighty proof. Light a match and the whole block goes up in flames.

I use my suitcase as a shield. He wields the balls like a medieval mace and leaves big dents in the leather. I could go for my gun, but blowing away a local on my first night in Santa Paulina might make a bad first impression.

Angel sees the patrol car before I do and flags it down. The officer bolts from the car, handcuffs at the ready, rain filling the brim of his cap. He's big, red Irish, with the kind of pale skin you don't parade in the summer sun.

'Drop the weapon like a good fellow, Elmer,' he says. 'I'll give you a nice dry place to sleep it off.'

The cop wears heavy gloves and drops the cuffs. He bends to pick them up and Elmer winds up for a head shot. I step in and snatch away the weapon before it picks up momentum. Red straightens up.

'That wasn't very nice,' he says and lands a good one to Elmer's solar plexus.

Elmer's wind abandons his chest with a noisy honk. His eyes roll into his head and he drops like a stone.

Red gives me a nod.

'Come on, mate,' he says. 'Grab an arm and we'll tuck him in for the night.'

We dump him beneath a striped awning against the pawnshop wall. Red reaches out to shake my hand but my back seizes. I stumble into him and he feels the gun. We size each other up and sense a primal bond, like wolves when they recognize a member of their own pack.

'You okay?' he asks.

'He got me a good one with those damn balls,' I say, tossing the weapon on the pawnshop roof. 'I'll be okay after a hot bath and a good night's sleep.'

I extend my hand.

'I'm Jim Tunney, S.P.P.D.,' he says.

'Jack Dunning, B.P.D., retired.'

'Bakersfield?'

'Boston.'

Angel's beside me again, her hand in the crook of my arm.

'I thought you talked funny,' he says good-naturedly. 'You could have plugged that guy and we'd be the better for it.'

'Someone will sooner than later.'

'You must be Hank's new security guy.'

'Word sure gets around.'

'No secrets in Little Ireland.' He nods toward the car. 'Come on, you two, get in.'

'What about him?' I say, indicating the guy snoring under the awning.

'He'll be fine. When he wakes up he won't remember any of this.'

I grab my suitcase. The umbrella's somewhere in Timbuktu.

We cross Dublin and Kildare Streets and he drops us off in front of The Rexford. We agree to get together for a drink once I'm settled. I sense the change in Angel Doll the minute we walk into the lobby of the hotel. A man seated in a chair against the wall looks over his racing form with eyes the color of bullets. Except for the white tie and hatband, he's completely in black. He has high cheekbones and a nose that's straight and sharp enough to cut paper.

Without a word Angel pulls away from me and takes the elevator to the second floor. The guy gives me a smirk. I've got plenty of time to knock it off his kisser so I let it ride.

The lobby of The Rexford looks like a million lobbies in a million towns. It has comfortable leather chairs on an oriental carpet sporting the requisite number of cigarette burns. There's a scattering of potted palms, tables for magazines and newspapers, and several art deco sand buckets bristling with cigarette butts.

The men who sit in the chairs look like a million men in a million towns: boxers from the local gym, racetrack devotees, factory workers, and pensioners down on their luck.

Hank looks up from behind the reception desk and gives me a welcoming nod. He's older and grayer than the last time I saw him. I walk over and slap him on the shoulder.

'You old son-of-a-gun,' I say. 'Looks like you've done okay for yourself.'

'It's not the Ritz, but it keeps me in brandy and cigars.'

My back cramps. I lean an elbow on the counter and blow out my breath.

'Some crazy s.o.b. blind-sided me with a sock of billiard balls.' I shake off the pain and straighten up.

'That's Elmer Ganguzza's game. He's the town nut. His mother drank too much when he was baking in the oven. I can have Doc McBane here in ten minutes.'

'Let's see how I feel in the morning. Right now I'm beat.'

'Take the weekend off and see how you feel on Monday.'

'Sounds like a plan. By the way, who's the skeleton with the racing form?'

'That's Axel Teague. As soon as you turned your back he followed the girl up the elevator. I wouldn't turn your back on him again if you catch my drift.'

Hank opens his desk drawer. I recognize the envelope he hands me. It's my termination check from the Department. I rip it open. It's not like I've won the Irish Sweepstakes, but it's enough to keep the wolf from the door.

'Want me to cash it?' asks Hank.

'Sure thing.'

I sign the back and he doles out the cash.

'I'd think twice about the girl if you want to keep your life uncomplicated,' says Hank. 'Teague has his brand on that one.'

Who wants to think? I want to hold her close and slow-dance in the smoky darkness. If Teague has similar aspirations we're probably not going to be best friends.

* * *

My key goes to a corner room with a small private bath. It's comfortable and clean. The pink and purple neon from the movie theater across Cork Street reflects on the ceiling. After I loosen my muscles with a hot shower I wrap a towel around my hips, some of the tightness gone out of my back. I'm on my way to bed when there's a knock on the door.

Angel says, 'Jack, it's me.'

I open the door. She steps inside and I lock it behind her. An angry bruise decorates her cheekbone.

I tilt her chin up and examine the damage.

'What's his hold on you?' I say.

She draws a trembling breath and I kiss her lightly on the temple.

'I've been with Teague since I was thirteen. He showed up with legal-looking papers when my parents died and said I had to go with him, that he was a distant relative. By the time I realized what was going on, I was trapped. He lives off of me and the other girls from The Blue Rose who work the streets.'

'What room is he in? This is the kind of riffraff I've been hired to deal with.'

'It doesn't matter. He won't be back until Monday after he's gambled his money away.' Angel turns toward the door. The wind is up and rain rattles the windowpane. 'I have to go. If I don't meet my quota, there'll be hell to pay when he gets back.'

I block the door. I remove one of the larger bills from my wallet and put it in her beaded purse. 'You don't have to do this. I took this job so people can be safe here.' She turns to me and slowly begins unbuttoning the pearl buttons on her blue dress.

'No, Angel,' and I begin fastening her dress.

She presses her fingers to my lips.

'Don't say a word, Jack.'

The dress slides off of her shoulders with the soft whisper of silk. She steps out of her shoes and I realize how very small she is. Another subtle shrug and she's wrapped in nothing but the pale translucence of her skin.

She reaches out and pulls the towel from my hips, takes me by the hand, and leads me to the bed. Her perfumed hair falls over my face, her body warm and firm against my chest. She's far too young or I'm far too old, however you want to look at it, but the chemistry is too strong to resist and it's been a long time since anyone has wanted me in this way.

Her soft, full lips find mine, but when I close my eyes it's another time, another

13

place, even another woman. I try to get Sandra out of my head but she drifts between us like a ghost. I'm suddenly twenty-three again and she's seventeen. We make love on a hillside beneath a summer moon, exhilarated and terrified at our recklessness. Sandra was my first and only love, until I ruined it.

Afterward I light two Luckys and watch the purple smoke dissolve in the shadows of the room. Lightning flickers beyond the window and thunder rolls across the roof. Angel turns on her side, one hand in my hair, the other holding her cigarette. Her sandy blonde hair spills across the pillow.

'Are you married?' she asks.

'She's divorcing me,' I say.

'Did you cheat on her?'

'Only with Jack Daniels.'

She looks in my eyes and I look away.

'I think you're still married under the skin,' she says, kissing me on the cheek. I sense her sadness, but she covers it with a smile.

★　★　★

I wake to a rainy morning. Angel's gone back to her room. She leaves a comforting warmth in the bedding, a whisper of rose perfume on the pillow.

The pain in my back returns in spades, running down my leg and into my toes. I soak in the tub and imagine shoving billiard balls down Ganguzza's throat.

It's Saturday. We want to be together, but it won't work as long as Teague is hovering in the halls of The Rexford like dry rot in the walls. Hank tells me a guy like that must have a past . . . a record . . . a warrant . . . something. He shows me his rental application. He's originally from Kansas City. The rest of the information is sketchy.

'I hired you to weed out the riffraff,' says Hank. 'Can't think of a better place to start.'

'I know just the guy to help me with that.' I call Jim at the precinct. He says he'll do some checking and get back to me.

Angel and I have pancakes and coffee at The Memory Lights Café on the corner of Shannon and Cork. She wears a

15

blue plastic raincoat and matching boots, her sunny hair long and flowing and dotted with raindrops. I pay the check and we hurry back up the street to catch the new Jean Harlow movie.

We laugh, eat popcorn, and drink Coke. Today I'm happy. I don't feel like a broken-down cop with a soon-to-be ex-wife who hates him. With Angel at my side I have a second chance to do things right, maybe even kick the booze. Then again, maybe not.

The curtain comes down on the double feature. It's after dark and we're back on the sidewalk. The neon lights from the marquee turn the raindrops pink and silver. Across the street in a recessed entryway down from the hotel, a ruby eye glows from the shadows. It could be some Joe ducking out of the rain for a smoke. It could also be Teague watching us. I'd walk over and check it out if I were alone, but Angel is chattering about the movie, asking if she should bleach and bob her hair like a Hollywood movie star. Why ruin the moment by starting a ruckus? Teague's not going anywhere. Neither am I.

Our evening comes to an end. Angel puts on a pink taffeta dress, matching shoes and a string of dime store pearls. She stands in front of the mirror, puts on earrings and a dab of perfume. She catches me watching her and smiles.

'Don't go,' I say. 'I'll take care of you.'

'I'm just going to say good-bye to the girls.'

'Be careful. Come to my room when you get back.' She turns from the mirror.

'Oh Jack,' she says, her head resting on my chest, 'they say you can't fall in love this fast, but . . .'

I hold her at arm's length. Her eyes are bluer than rain.

'What do they know?'

We stand inside the doors of the lobby waiting for the taxi. I give her money for fare and kiss her on the curve of her neck. She laughs and says it tickles. She's beautiful when she laughs, when the sadness goes into hiding. The taxi pulls to the curb and she skips out the door. When I walk back through the lobby I can still smell her perfume.

Back in my room the phone rings. Hank patches Jim Tunney through. He says to go through the back entrance of the building next door. It was called The Zebra Room before Prohibition. Now it's the speakeasy where cops and attorneys get tanked. I leave a ten in my wallet and put the rest of the bills in the top dresser drawer with my gun. Who needs a gun? I'm having drinks with a cop.

The doorman points to a red leather booth in the corner of the room. A bucket of beer and two chilled mugs sit on the table. I can tell from the look on Jim's face that he's got something for me.

'You dug up some dirt on Teague,' I say, sliding into the booth.

'And the deeper I dig, the darker it gets.'

'So, what's his résumé?' I say, filling my mug. I shift my weight on the bench. That's all it takes to ratchet up the pain in my back. This isn't an injury that's going to resolve itself overnight.

'He was in Kansas City until four years ago,' he says. 'Big-time pimp. Seems that every hooker who wanted out of his stable

18

ended up in the river with their hands tied behind their back. Same thing if they had the audacity to get pregnant or pick up some unfortunate disease. Believe me, you don't want to know the gruesome details.'

'So, how come he's not behind bars?'

'He skipped town and drove west before homicide had a solid case. Dead girls don't talk and the live ones are afraid to.'

'Where does that leave us? Are you saying he's untouchable?'

'He's wanted for questioning on the homicides, but there's no law says you have to talk with the police. He was, however, a no-show on a court date for pandering, so they put out a bench warrant.'

I light a cigarette and pour another mug of beer.

'Maybe you could have him extradited.'

'I can call Kansas City. I bet we can rattle his cage.'

'Angel wants out. He's not going to take it well.'

'I'll get on it first thing Monday morning.'

We smoke up the room and finish another bucket of beer. I pay the tab and cross the alley to The Rexford. I'm buzzed and my throat's raw. A day in Santa Paulina and I have a job, a girl, two friends and an enemy. What more can a guy ask for? I walk into the lobby. Hank is in the middle of the room headed toward the door.

'Jesus, Jack. I was just coming to get you. All hell broke loose about a minute ago. It's Angel. Teague worked her over real bad. Her clothes are ripped. She has a terrible bite on her arm. I tried to steer her next door but she's already gone up the elevator.'

I hobble up stairs I'd normally have taken two at a time, three on a good day. I reach the second story landing, calling her name.

The door to my room is open. Pearls from her necklace are scattered across the floor. The dresser drawer is upside down on the bed. My money is gone. My gun is gone. Angel Doll is gone.

The floor vibrates beneath my feet as the elevator returns to the lobby. I

20

scramble down the stairs and stumble into the wall. The nerve in my back is on fire.

Hank is waiting at the bottom of the stairs.

'She jumped in a taxi going west on Cork.'

'Where the hell to?'

'Probably the midnight train to L.A. You've got maybe fifteen minutes before it pulls out.' Hank hurries over and reaches behind the counter. 'Jack,' he calls and tosses me a set of car keys. 'It's the black Ford Coupe out back. Go west on Cork. A mile after you cross the bridge, turn right on Depot Street.'

2

Showdown at Midnight

I gun down Cork in the midnight rain, the windshield wipers working overtime, the tires hissing over the asphalt. I fly past the Rescue Mission, Sal's Pawn-shop, and The Blue Rose Dance Hall. I clatter over the Santa Paulina Bridge, the water black and raging one hundred feet below. When I get to Depot Street I snap a sharp right and slide up to the platform.

Passengers fold their umbrellas as they file into the train. A few turn their heads to watch the stone-faced man in black dragging the lady away from the tracks. The women avert their eyes. The men are afraid to get involved.

Teague drags Angel across the platform toward a black Caddy whose driver's side door is open, like this is going to be an easy grab. I guess it's up to me to screw up his plan. I get out of the Ford. Angel sees me.

'Jack!' she cries, 'Jack!'

The blue raincoat is missing a few buttons. The sleeve is torn, exposing an angry bite mark. She's lost a pink shoe and one of her pearl earrings.

At the sound of my name, Teague turns toward me with a sneer. With my gimpy leg I look about as threatening as road kill.

'Don't waste your time,' he says. 'You've had your free roll in the hay. I've got legal custody of this little tramp.' He holds her tightly by the wrist. She struggles, her hair a golden tangle in the light above the station door.

The stationmaster pokes his head out of the ticket window.

'We got trouble here, mister?'

'Call the precinct,' I say. 'This man is wanted for murder.'

'Like hell I am!' snaps Teague.

The stationmaster pulls his head back inside and slams the window closed.

I'm not in fighting form. No one knows that better than I do. If Hank has connected with Tunney, he could be here any minute. If not it'll take the city cops about ten minutes once they leave the station.

I limp to Teague's Caddy. Nice car. New and shiny. I reach inside. It smells like a new pair of Italian leather shoes. I switch off the engine.

'What the hell are you doing?' he says.

I fling the keys into the darkness like I'm on the pitching mound in the big leagues. His arrogance slips a notch. In his moment of distraction, Angel Doll slams him in the head with her purse. His hat tumbles away and she twists free, backing away from him as I advance.

I power-limp across the platform. Teague swivels toward Angel and slams her to her knees with a bunched fist. In the second it takes him to gloat, I land a good one to his jaw. I hear a satisfying snap . . . a tooth . . . maybe a bone. I can't strut like a horny rooster, but there's iron in my fist.

'You son of a bitch,' he says, and comes at me hard. His shoe slams my ribcage.

Cartilage rips from the bone and I stagger sideways.

Angel screams as she watches me struggle to stay on my feet. My body clenches around the pain. I hear a distant siren. Jim should be here in two minutes, maybe three. Either way, Teague isn't going anywhere without a car.

Teague gives me a bloody, broken-toothed smile. A straight razor materializes in his right hand. I have nothing to lose, so I make one final play. Where I come from, if you gotta go down, you go down fighting. He thrusts toward my gut and I grab for the weapon. Angel rises to her feet. I'll never know how successful my effort would have been, because a bullet whines past my ear and the razor clatters to the wooden planks.

Teague needs both hands to plug the hole in his throat. He's sprung a sizeable leak and blood dribbles between his fingers. He looks surprised, like how can so sterling a fellow as himself come to such an ignoble end? He drops to his knees with a gurgle, falls forward on his face and bleeds out on the boards.

Angel looks down at him with the gun in her hand. My gun. One of her eyes is swollen closed and a bruise is spreading across her cheekbone. She doesn't seem to comprehend what has just happened.

'It's all right,' I say. 'Hand me the gun.'

She looks at me with a dazed expression, like she's doesn't know who I am, like I'm a stranger who's wandered onto the scene. I take a step toward her and she takes a step back. The gun is heavy and her arm falls to her side.

The whistle blows. Cars begin inching down the tracks.

'Angel, everything is going to be okay. We can clear this whole thing up.'

Patrol cars pull onto Depot Street. The train moves slowly over rails that are silver with rain. Angel looks at the train, then at me, then at the train again.

'Angel,' I say, but she's in a dead zone beyond my orbit.

She drops the gun and runs along the platform as the train picks up speed. I start after her, but my leg buckles and I go down. She raises her arm. A hand reaches downward and grabs her wrist.

She's briefly suspended in air, then disappears inside the train. My last vision of Angel is her tear-stained face at the window and her little hand pressed against the glass as the train picks up speed.

I'm pulled to my feet by a strong hand. It's Jim. He walks over and pockets the gun, then looks down at the body, his face expressionless. I throw my weight on my good leg. A second patrol car pulls up to the depot. Two young officers climb onto the platform and out of the rain.

'Duggan,' says Jim, 'see that the Ford gets back to Hank Featherstone at The Rexford? This gentleman is too injured to drive.'

'Yes sir.' Duggan can't take his eyes off the body. I'm not sure that any of us have seen that much blood in one place at one time.

'Duggan — now, if you don't mind,' says Jim.

'The keys are in the ignition,' I say. He walks off looking a little green around the gills.

The other officer stands waiting for orders.

'Boyle, forget the ambulance and get the coroner down here.'

'Right away, sir. Do you know who's responsible for all this . . . blood?'

'Mr. Dunning seems to be the only witness. I'll see what he has to say.'

'Who's the victim?'

'There is no victim. That's Axel Teague.'

Boyle scratches his head. 'If there's no victim, there's no perp.'

'You get smarter every day, Boyle,' he says, and bags the razor for evidence.

★ ★ ★

Jim stops the car on the bridge. The night is dense and black and the river roaring. He takes my gun out of his pocket and tosses it over the railing.

'So there won't be any questions later,' he says. 'The way I see it . . . no girl . . . no gun . . . no sweat. Got a problem with that?'

'That's the way I'd tell it,' I say.

We drive in silence for a while with rain pounding on the roof of the car.

'Jack,' he says, 'a word of advice. Don't obsess over the girl. Sure, you could follow her to L.A., but believe me, by the time you find her she won't be alone.'

'Aren't you a little ray of sunshine,' I say.

He sputters a laugh. There's the trace of a smile on my lips, not because things are funny — just at the crap life throws at you. We pass The Blue Rose Dance Hall. The door swings open and Elmer Ganguzza sails through the air and lands on the sidewalk. Water pours off the windshield and Jim turns the wipers on high.

'Whether it's Boston or Santa Paulina, some things never change,' I say.

'You don't say . . . Speaking of Boston, ever work cold cases?'

'Sure, I've worked my share.'

'The Chief's going to do some snooping into your solve record at B.P.D. If he likes what he sees, he's going to ask you to have a look at some of our old cases. He'd like to put you on as a consultant. Isn't every day we run across a big city cop. It shouldn't interfere with

29

what you've got going at The Rexford and a guy can always use a few extra bucks.'

I'm about to tell a whopper, then I figure what the hell.

'Before I sign on you should know they canned my butt in Boston because I drink too much. I'm still on the bottle.'

'Too much is a relative term. The Chief says if you don't fall off the floor you haven't exceeded your limit. You two should get along just fine.'

'Let's talk again on Monday,' I say. 'All I can think about right now is a stiff drink and a warm sack.'

★   ★   ★

I guess I'm moaning in my sleep because Hank calls in the doc about 3:00 a.m. and I hear them talking in the hall outside my door.

'You got to do something, Doc. No one can get any sleep with all that moaning and groaning.'

'I'll take a shot at it,' says McBane.

He zaps me in the hip with a syringe the size of a rolling pin and the pain melts away like warm candle wax.

Alone in my room I down a shot of Jack Daniels and savor the mellow burn. I listen to the rain tick against the windowpane and watch the reflections of neon ripple across the ceiling. I've had one hell of a welcome to my new town.

I light the last Lucky in the pack and think of Angel and how her pale velvet skin felt against mine. I think of her soft hair on my cheek and the intoxicating waves of her perfume. One glorious night together and what do I have to show for it? A broken string of dime store pearls and an empty wallet. It's not that funny, but I can't help smiling.

'They say you can't fall in love this fast,' said Angel Doll. Maybe not, but what we had was a damn good facsimile. She couldn't take the place of Sandra . . . no one could . . . but, she was one hell of a fix for a lonely guy with a bum leg.

Angel Doll is getting off the train in L.A. about now. She'll be wearing a torn blue raincoat and one pink shoe. She'll have enough money for a little food and a week or two in a hotel, provided it's near

31

the Greyhound Station and she doesn't mind sharing a bathroom down the hall with washed-up hookers and derelicts.

Then again, with her angel face, she might nail a rich guy or a married businessman who can afford to keep a woman on the side. I wonder where she'll be in a month or a year.

I wonder if she will ever think of me.

★   ★   ★

Five-fifteen on Saturday evening, and Joseph Crisalli puts the rest of the glazed donuts in a box and climbs the indoor staircase to Madame Zarina's apartment above the bakery.

'Cookie, it's Joe,' he calls.

To Joe, she's Cathleen Cook. They went to parochial school together more years ago than he cares to recall. In the ensuing forty years they married other people, watched children leave home and spouses pass away. They also became best friends.

Her door opens before he reaches the top step. Her right eye is red and

32

unfocused but she still manages a smile.

'Not the migraine again,' he says, touching her hand.

'When I was a kid, my doctor said I might outgrow them, but at sixty-five, I don't think that's going to happen.'

As a child she was knocked unconscious in a buckboard accident and has suffered with migraines ever since. She doesn't get them often, but when she does, she has visions in her sleep that have no resemblance to ordinary dreams. They are insights into violent deaths of people she's never met or heard of.

'Is there anything I can do, dear?' he asks.

'I wish there was, Joe.'

'If you need to go to the hospital, promise to call me and I'll drive you.'

'I do promise, old boy.'

'I think you just accepted my proposal,' he says. 'I've been waiting to hear those words for years.'

She punches him playfully on the arm, but the small gesture makes her head pound and she leans against the door-frame.

'Off with you now,' she says. 'I'll see you on Monday.'

'I'll leave these with you.' He hands her the pink bakery box. 'I hope you feel better in the morning.'

He goes down the stairs. She hears the bell jingle above the door as he goes out and locks up for the night. Joe is a comforting presence. She feels a bit lonely after he's gone, like the temperature in the room has dropped a degree or two. She steps inside and closes the door.

Joe looks up at Cookie's window through the rain-washed darkness. The sign below the sill reads:

MADAME ZARINA
FORTUNES TOLD FOR A DIME

He doesn't envy Cookie the dubious gift that has been visited upon her by the gods of calamity. He wonders what poor soul will die on this cold night at the tag end of the year. He makes the sign of the cross like he's done since he was a small boy at St. Finnbar's. He looks in the rear-view mirror, pulls into the street and heads toward home, home being that big empty house on the edge of town where his cat waits for him in the window.

★ ★ ★

Cookie turns out all the lights except the lamp in the front window with the red glass shade. When she's in the grip of a migraine, every light is too bright and every sound too loud. She walks through the parlor where an over-stuffed sofa and easy chair rest on an oriental carpet. Heavy red drapes are fastened with gold tassels and on a round table in the center of the room; her crystal ball sits on a cloth of midnight blue brocade. There's a grandfather clock in the corner and Maxfield Parrish prints on the papered walls.

The waves of nausea and dizziness that accompany the pain propel her toward the bedroom. She drinks her medication from a demitasse and changes into a white nightgown with high neck and long sleeves. As she sinks onto the canopy bed with its purple veils emblazoned with gold stars, she knows it will not be for a good night's sleep.

Dr. McBane says only childbirth and kidney stones come close to the pain of a migraine headache. He's never charged her for the mysterious potion he drops in her purse when her head is turned. An opiate perhaps, since he doesn't acknowledge dispensing it and she knows better than to ask.

The medicine works quickly, dropping her down the fathomless well of sleep. At first there's only darkness and the sound of blood rushing through her ears as she sinks beneath layers of receding consciousness. Then her inner eye opens like the lens of a camera on an unfamiliar landscape.

The vision has begun.

The wind and rain thrash the treetops, sending leaves and brittle twigs showering downward. A young woman carrying a hand-woven basket runs into the dream-frame. She loses her hat to a low-hanging branch. Her dark brown hair whips around her head like the mane of a horse. A vine reaches out to snag her toe and she lands on her hands and knees in the leaf litter, the contents of the basket scattering across the forest floor.

A second person enters the frame wearing a big coat and carrying a knife. The scream of the fallen girl cuts across the warp of the wind like a bottle shattering against a rock. A heavy boot slams several times into her back and head.

Raindrops glisten on the metal surface of the knife. The assailant drops to one knee and rolls her over to look at her face, the beautiful unconscious face that causes so much trouble. Now for a kiss on those cold, blue lips — not a lover's kiss, but a kiss to seal a deadly deed. The knife plunges down again and again through the girl's patched winter coat, blood oozing through the slashes.

The hair on the back of the assailant's neck rises like the hackles of a billy goat, every nerve on edge. Someone is watching. Wary eyes scan the surrounding woods and see nothing, but that doesn't mean that someone isn't there. What the attacker doesn't know is that Zarina the

Fortune Teller is watching every move.

Cookie tries to see the face of the attacker but the vision is losing definition, like the image on an over-exposed photograph. The murderer runs into the woods and disappears from view.

Cookie can't take her eyes from the girl on the forest floor, from the serene face washed clean by the rain. Her eyes are closed, like a saint in repose. Rain soaks through her bloody clothes and drenches the long tresses of her hair.

The young lady's eyes open, wide green eyes with yellow flecks in the iris, eyes that reflect the sky. They gaze unblinking into the treetops. She doesn't move because she can't. Something is broken in her back.

There's a sound like a needle scratching the surface of a record and the vision is gone. Cookie sits up in bed, her head swirling with pain, her heart stuttering erratically. She fumbles for the vial of nitroglycerin on the nightstand and places a pill beneath her tongue until the rhythm evens out.

Tonight's vision is different from the

others, full of gaps and voids. More importantly, this victim isn't dead. This is a first. She knows neither the name of the victim, the identity of the perpetrator nor the location of the crime. Miserable and frustrated, she drops back on her pillow.

*　　*　　*

Sunday morning and the headache is gone, leaving a visible bruising around one eye and a delicate webbing of red capillaries in the white. Cookie sits at the table with her coffee and donuts, her hands moving over the smooth surface of the crystal ball as if it actually had insight into life's dilemmas.

Cookie has unashamedly admitted to Joe that her crystal ball is no more than the focal point of her intuitive energies. It has no psychic or magical powers to impart. On the other hand, she's no phony. People come to her when their concerns overwhelm them and leave feeling less lonely and more in control of their lives. She's been privy to more sins and secrets than Father Doyle at St.

Finnbar's or Chief Garvey down at the station. People are more inclined to open up to someone who lacks the power or the inclination to relegate them to hell or jail.

Cookie looks out the window at the rain falling on Cork St. This morning she has a dilemma. Years ago, she led police to the lifeless body of three-year-old Bucky Chapelle. It was revealed in a vision that he'd had been beaten to death and hidden in a culvert on Silver Creek. Rather than gratitude, she was suspected of complicity in the crime. How could she know so much if she hadn't been part of it? She was exonerated when Bucky's stepfather confessed to 'maybe going overboard' when he disciplined the boy for dropping his pack of cigarettes in the toilet. After that, she kept her visions to herself.

She didn't call the station about the waitress who disappeared two years back. They found her remains in a ditch near the city dump where Cookie knew she'd been since day one. Nor did she call when she envisioned thirteen-year-old Gretchen

Frey give birth to a baby girl at home and extinguish the child's brief flame of life. The remains were discovered buried under the floor of the chicken coop six months later. Whether Cookie reported these incidents or not, the victims wouldn't have been any less dead, but the young lady in the woods was different. She was alive.

*   *   *

Sergeants Don Swackhammer and Bruce Green are on duty at the station. Sundays, especially rainy ones, are quiet. The troublemakers who frequent the watering holes of Santa Paulina on Saturday nights are home nursing black eyes and hangovers and trying to recall the name of the woman in the bed beside them. That is hunky-dory with Don and Bruce, who are both as lazy as hell and won't take accident reports in bad weather unless serious injuries are involved.

The Chief is home with his wife and six kids, so they put their feet up on the desks and kick back with their auto, hunting and spicy magazines, drink coffee, smoke and tell jokes. Oh yes, life is good until the phone rings. Nobody wants to pick up no matter who's on the other end, each hoping to outwait the other. Don finally caves in.

'Officer Swackhammer. What can I do for ya?'

'Good morning, Officer. This is Cathleen Cook.

Madame Zarina. Wouldn't you know it! Don looks over at Bruce, mouths her name and rolls his eyes. Bruce chuckles silently. He can rib Don for a week on this one.

'Yes, Madame Zarina, I'm listening. A young lady injured in the woods? Really? The victim of foul play. No, I can't say anyone has reported a girl missing. Yes, of course I'm taking notes.'

'Without a pen in your hand, Officer?'

'Well . . . I . . . how?'

'Not everything requires a crystal ball, Officer Swackhammer,' she says. 'Does the Chief know you're scuffing up public property with those cowboy boots of yours?' Don looks around like she might be peeking through the window, thumps his feet to the floor and picks up a pencil. How in hell does the old biddy know?

'There, isn't that better?'

For the next few minutes he dutifully takes down every word. When she's safely off the line, he crumples up the note and tosses it in the wastepaper basket.

'What are you doing?' asks Bruce.

'She's talking crazy about some girl been attacked in the woods. I don't know what she expects us to do about it.'

'She see it happen?'

'Dreamed it. Ain't like real evidence. Now, if we had a missing persons report it might carry a little weight.' He wipes a drip of tobacco juice from the side of his mouth and spits into the wastepaper basket.

'I don't know, Don. A lot of folks around here swear by them visions of hers. She told my sister her husband was going to leave her before Thanksgiving and it came true.'

'Anybody could have figured that one out the way he's been carrying on with

that cocktail waitress from the Lepre-
chaun Lounge.'

'I guess you're right. Here, you want to
read a good article about fly fishing on
the Klamath?'

3

Earning My Keep

Whatever the doc shot me up with erased Sunday from the calendar of memory. It's still raining. I'm out of cigarettes and booze. The other side of the bed, so warm and inviting a few days ago, is cold. I turn over and breathe in Angel's scent from the pillow, knowing even that will soon be gone.

Jim gave me good advice, but I'm not smart enough to take it. I'm smart about a lot of things, but women isn't one of them. 'Let her go,' he says. 'Write her off.' If I do, it makes a fraud of what we shared. I swallowed a hook and it lodged deep in my heart.

I obsess about Angel. I'm a hopeless case when it comes to the women in my life. Hell, I can't even stop thinking about Sandra, who sleeps next to my replacement on what was once my side of the bed.

Angel is not Sandra.

My soon-to-be ex-wife is sophisticated and worldly-wise. She can take care of herself, probably better now that I'm out of the way. But, Angel is alone for the first time in her life. Despite her hardships she's still as sweet and soft-centered as a bon-bon in a candy box.

I will find her and it has to be before L.A. chews her up and spits her out, before she ends up with the wrong people doing the wrong things. But, L.A. is a big place, I don't know my way around the city and I haven't decided where best to begin.

The doc shows up on his way to the hospital. He tells me I have a severe case of sciatica. These things are tricky. It might get better. It might not. I could have made the same prognosis and saved two bucks. I pay him. He leaves me with a bottle of pain pills and tells me not to take too many.

'How many is too many?'

'If you end up in the morgue, you'll

need to cut down.'

He laughs at his joke as he goes out the door.

The city beyond my window is depressing. Rain drizzles down the pane. A draft leaks in around the sash. This is not the California of postcards. No beaches. No palm trees. No gingerbread tans.

I'm craving a morning smoke when a newsboy knocks on my door. He's a cute little squirt named Albie. I buy a copy of the Santa Paulina *Morning Sun*. Albie runs errands for tips so I give him a dime to go to the lobby and get me a pack of cigarettes from the machine. He jingles the nickel tip in with the rest of his morning take. The kid's okay, says he makes the rounds again at five-thirty if I want to order from the café. After he leaves I smoke two cigarettes, take a couple pills and go through the paper looking for an article on the shooting. I find it on page two. It has Jim's fingerprints all over it.

LOCAL MOBSTER GUNNED DOWN BY UNKNOWN RIVAL.

That's all I need to know.

I shower, shave and make it to the lobby by eight. It's full of readers and smokers working on the free coffee and donuts set out on the front desk. A floor model radio is tuned to the news. There's the rustle of paper and the occasional cigarette cough.

'I'll introduce you around a little later, give people a chance to wake up first,' says Hank. 'The leg any better this morning?'

'We'll see. The doc fixed me up with some pills.'

'That's good. He treats boxing injuries down at Duffy's Gym. There's not much going on right now. I can give you a stack of rental apps to take back to your room. The tenants are already installed but you can see if any red flags go up.'

'Sounds like a plan.'

He goes to the cabinet behind the desk and hands me a stack of files. I grab a donut and a cup of coffee and walk to the plate glass window that overlooks Cork St. The theater is dark. The only person I see is a homeless man pushing a shopping cart against a stiff headwind. Water rushes down the flooded gutters, the green traffic light on the corner of Cork and Avalon dancing in the ripples. At least I don't have to shovel my way to the sidewalk like I did in Boston.

I walk to the elevator and push the button with my elbow. The cage rattles me to the second floor. The sound brings back unwelcome memories of the night everything went to hell.

There's an easy chair and a decent reading lamp by my window. I set my coffee and ashtray on the table beside it and take a cursory glance through the stack of applications. When I'm finished I scrutinize each one individually.

Most of the people at The Rexford are decent types. Many have restaurant or cannery jobs. Others lost their homes to the dust storms or foreclosure and came to California looking for a better life. There are veterans of the Great War, and a punch-drunk boxer; Hank allows them to live rent-free.

Then there are the handful of men and women with a skeleton or two they'd like to keep from leaping out of the closet. What they leave off of their applications is more telling than what they include. Some are running from bench warrants in other jurisdictions, avoiding child support or alimony. Others are escaping abusive husbands or shady pasts. If they pay their rent and don't cause a ruckus I have no intention of upsetting their apple carts. It's the Axel Teagues that concern me — not that I'd recommend shooting them. With Teague it just worked out that way.

Seeing no red flags, I return the applications to Hank. He locks them back in the file cabinet, then gives me a tour of the hotel, introducing me to the tenants we bump into along the way. I meet the janitorial and housekeeping staff and get the general lay of the land.

It's not a large hotel, only three floors above the lobby, twenty rooms per floor. There are few vacancies: two on the third, 216 where Angel lived, 318 where Teague hung his hat and 310 where ninety-year-old Dobie Gunderson passed away.

Now that my leg is holding up I'm out

to earn my keep. I tell Jake Sherman, the head janitor, that I'll help him clean out 310. He's a pleasant fiftyish black man who plays sax at Smokey's Fire Pit on Saturday nights. He's also Albie's dad. There had been a Mrs. Sherman, but she bailed out when the going got tough.

Jake and Albie live down in the furnace room, which isn't as bad as it sounds. They have twin beds in an alcove beneath the ductwork. There's a bathroom at one end and the communal laundry room at the other. It's warm in winter, cool in summer and it's free.

Jake says Mr. Gunderson outlived his wife, his five kids and all of his old friends. 'A man can die too young,' he says, 'like all them boys in the Big War, but a man can also outlive his capacity to enjoy his existence.'

Who can argue with that? I like Jake. He's smart. An armchair philosopher. We can use a little philosophy these days.

Gunderson's room is comfortable but sparse. He doesn't have a lot of stuff, but he took good care of what he had. We find a box of family photos . . . financial records . . . a journal . . . love letters from his youth. We consign the contents to the basement furnace because there's no one left to take them, no one who remembers his smile, his disappointments and victories. That leaves some clothes, towels, a flowered bedspread and toiletries. Jake asks can he load the things in his truck and deliver them to the Hooverville where the folks from his church help out.

I say, if it's okay with Hank it's okay with me.

Jake knows my history with Angel and Teague. I guess everybody does, the way word gets around. He gathers up the hand-me-downs and we go down the hall in opposite directions so I can go through their rooms in private. I take my passkey and enter 318. I can't wait to toss Teague's room. If Saturday night had gone the other way, he'd be tossing mine.

I find a gun under his mattress and pocket it. He owes me for the one Jim tossed off the bridge. In the back of the closet is a moneybox heavy with paper currency and coins, probably from gambling, loan-sharking and the money made off the backs of the girls from The Blue Rose. There's a gold pocket watch, two jewel-movement wristwatches, a diamond pinky ring and an emerald horseshoe stickpin. You wear that prissy crap in the neighborhood I was raised in and the 'real' guys kick the hell out of you. I set the valuables aside for Hank. It'll make up for Teague vacating without the requisite 30 days' notice.

In the bedside stand I find a cloisonné snuffbox, and after a moment of indecision, flush the cocaine inside down the toilet. I have no reservations, however, when it comes to the carton of cigarettes and the unopened bottle of expensive brandy.

His closet yields what I expect: expensive sharkskin suits, silk shirts, fancy fedoras and shiny shoes . . . all black to match his heart. No documents, personal papers or letters, like the guy who has no future also had no past.

I bring Hank the valuables. He sends three tall, skinny guys up to Teague's room. They return looking snappy as hell in their new outfits. Black from head to toe. They give a fashion show in the lobby. We all laugh and call them the three morticians.

I take the elevator to the second floor. It's my first time in Angel's room. The shade is down. I stand in the amber gloom, take a deep breath and let it out.

There's a white coverlet on the bed, everything neat and clean, a vague hint of perfume and cigarette residue in the air. I go to the window at the back of the room overlooking the alley and raise the shade. The roofs of cars outside the back entrance glitter in the rain, a wet dog picks through an overturned garbage can and a trio of electrical wires snap in the wind between the poles. I watch raindrops slide down the pane and wonder how my best intentions led to such a disastrous outcome.

In the closet is the blue dress Angel wore when we danced to 'Stormy Weather'. There's a couple hats, a few pairs of shoes, just enough things for a girl to get by. On the top of the dressing table is a light dusting of spilled powder, three tubes of pink lipstick, a half-pack of cigarettes, a charm bracelet, a bottle of perfume and a sadly prophetic dime novel called *Love and Bullets*. In the drawer are combs, bobby pins and curlers.

I move to the bureau and open the left top drawer. Included in a stack of papers I find letters tied with frayed pink ribbon and a birth certificate . . . hers.

ANGEL DAWN DAHL. D.O.B. DECEMBER 20, 1918.
PLACE OF BIRTH: BANNING, CALIFORNIA.
HAIR: BLONDE. EYES: BLUE.
MOTHER'S MAIDEN NAME: SIGRID JENSEN.
FATHER'S NAME: ROLF DAHL.

I open the top right-hand drawer. Lavender sachets are scattered among a rainbow of frilly underthings.

Regardless of Jim's world-weary observations, Angel is worth finding. She's worth whatever it takes . . . time . . . money . . . even a bullet. I close the drawer and lock up the room.

4

Perfect Prey

The train pulls into the station with an unnerving shriek of the whistle and a grinding of brakes. Angel peers through the dusty coach window, expecting to see a swarm of policemen waiting to haul her off to jail. She doesn't see any uniforms or badges, but that doesn't mean an officer isn't lurking around in plain clothes.

She can't believe she's a murderer on the run. She was only trying to save Jack from Teague's blade when the gun jumped to life in her hand. When a hole opened in Teague's throat, her mind went blank. She couldn't believe that she was alive and the man she feared was dead. Recalling the blood makes her light-headed. The conductor offers his hand and she steps from the train. She stands on the platform trying to decide what to do next.

'Move along, dear,' says a gentleman carrying a silver-tipped cane. She steps aside so people can pass. Everyone is greeted with smiles and warm embraces. Everyone else has nice traveling clothes.

A man looks over the top of his newspaper. He has an orange crew cut, a bad complexion and a thick neck roped with blue veins. He notices the young girl with the ripped coat and bruised face. His interest piques the longer she stands there looking like a lost puppy, one more pretty young thing running from abuse or coming to L.A. with movie star dreams. He folds his newspaper and watches from the predawn shadows.

Angel clings to her beaded purse. A nice lady on the train gave her a pair of black leather flats and pinned the sleeve of her coat so the bite didn't show. Others gave her furtive glances, then turned away when she caught them staring. She tosses the pink shoe and stray earring in a trashcan. What good is one shoe? What good is one earring?

Angel walks from the platform into the waiting room. At this hour it's nearly

57

empty. There's a high-beamed ceiling and tall windows. A child sleeps beside her mother on one of the polished oak benches. A few men read their morning papers. Her footsteps echo across the Spanish tile floor. She walks into a restaurant at the far end of the room and takes a table by the window. She can think more clearly once she's had a cup of coffee. The waitress brings a menu.

'Just coffee, please,' she says, knowing the money must stretch until she finds a job. When the coffee is poured Angel laces it liberally with cream and sugar for extra calories, remembering how hoboes who passed through Banning made soup by adding catsup to cups of hot water at the local café, those items being free for the taking.

She lifts the mirrored compact from her purse and powders her nose. It would be nice to have a hat with a floppy brim to hide her bruises. As Angel snaps her compact shut, she sees a man looking at her. He's very respectable-looking with movie star good looks. He wears a white summer suit and immaculate white shoes.

His dark hair is silver at the temples and his flawless skin is the color of milk chocolate. It's hard not to notice a man who looks like a matinee idol.

As Angel sips her coffee, the orange-haired man takes a chair at the table behind her. There's a loud clatter at the back of the room and every head swivels toward the noise. A waitress has collided with a child running in the aisle and the plates balanced on her arm clatter to the floor.

With Angel's attention focused on the back of the room, the man behind her rises from his seat. He strides past Angel's table and sweeps her purse under his paper. The man is trotting out of the restaurant, headed for the door that leads to the parking lot, when Angel realizes what has happened.

'Help! That man stole my purse. Somebody help me.'

The thief looks over his shoulder and breaks into a run. The gentleman in the white suit is already giving chase. Angel scrapes back her chair and follows. Outside on the sidewalk the gentleman catches up and grabs the thief by the back of his collar. The younger man bunches his fist, lands a blow to the side of the man's head and breaks free. The man in white staggers and Angel grabs his arm to keep him from falling. When she looks up, the thief has disappeared over a fence on the far side of the parking lot.

'Are you hurt?' she asks.

'I'll be all right in a moment,' he says, straightening his coat. 'I hope the family jewels were not in your handbag.'

She attempts a smile, but breaks into tears. Everything in her life seems to be going wrong.

'I'm sorry,' she says. 'All of my money is in that purse.'

'Then I have failed you miserably.' He studies her and rubs his chin. His eyes are soft and brown and very kind. 'My name is Ricardo Escobar. I was about to have breakfast. I'd be honored if you would be my guest.'

Angel isn't sure this is a good idea. Then again, she's hungry and has no idea how far she'll have to walk today.

'Yes, that would be nice,' she says.

'What shall I call you?'

'Angel, Angel Jensen,' she says, deciding quickly on her mother's maiden name.

'Yes, of course, you do have a Scandinavian look about you. It's refreshing to see light hair that hasn't come out of a bottle.' He sweeps his arm in a gallant gesture. 'Shall we?'

They settle into a booth as the dawn sky goes from dove gray to peach. They have bacon and eggs and finish with a last cup of coffee. Angel wants to be better company, but she's thinking about Jack — how they walked in the rain to the corner of Cork and Shannon and ate at The Memory Lights Café, went to the movies and talked and laughed. There isn't much to laugh about anymore.

The waitress leaves a check beside Rick's saucer. Even the waitress looks like a movie star. She has red upswept hair and cleverly made-up blue-green eyes. Rick looks down and picks up the check. With his attention focused elsewhere, she gives Angel an odd, rather unsettling look. The name tag securing the fluffy handkerchief to the bodice of her uniform reads, 'Marcella'. It's a very pretty name. Marcella looks as if she's about to speak when Rick looks up and the moment passes. She probably disapproves of Angel having breakfast with a stranger or wants to ask about her bruises. Everyone wants to know whether they ask or not, like when you see a man with one arm and wonder if it was lost in the war or in a car accident.

'Ready?' he asks with a smile.

'Yes, thank you. I feel so much better.' They walk to the cash register. He peels a new five from an alligator wallet fat with bills.

'Keep the change,' he says.

It must be comforting to be so assured of one's place in the world. Not like herself. Not like Jack with his complexities. Maybe that's why she and Jack belong together — two complex people in a complicated world.

'Come on,' he says. 'I'll drop you off.'

Not knowing what else to do, she follows him to the parking lot. After the cold and damp of Santa Paulina, the rising sun is like a benediction. The tops of palm trees sway in a warm breeze and somewhere nearby a church bell rings.

'So, where to, young lady? You have relatives in town?'

'No, I've actually come looking for work. There isn't much in the way of employment back home, just the fields and the cannery.'

'How have you been getting by?' he asks casually.

'My uncle took care of me, but he passed away recently. My parents died a few years ago.'

'You seem awfully young to be on your own.'

'Not that young. I was twenty-one on my last birthday.' She should have said eighteen. It would have been more believable, but once said, it can't be taken back. They arrive at the car. It's fancy and new. He opens the passenger-side door. She hesitates.

'Go ahead, get in. You can't get far without money, especially in this town. My daughter's away at university and left a closet of clothes she no longer wants. If you hope to get a job you must make the right impression.'

'I don't know . . . '

'Look at this face,' he says, and wiggles his eyebrows. 'Do I look like a hatchet murderer?' He does have a very nice face and he's taken a blow coming to her aid. Angel considers her limited options and climbs in. The door closes with the muffled click of an expensive jewelry box. Mr. Escobar walks around the front of the car, climbs in and puts on his sunglasses. The car smells brand new and she runs her fingers over the polished dash.

'What kind of car is this?' she asks. 'I've never seen one like it.'

'A Bentley. You'll see a few more around town.' After a pause, he says, 'I don't mean to be rude, but I can't help noticing your bruises.'

'It's nothing to worry about. I was in a rear-ender and hit my face on the dash.'

They cruise west into Hollywood and pull onto a street called Franklin, then right into the Hollywood Hills on Beachwood. The car climbs the narrow twisting roads, switching from one side street to another. The neighborhood is quiet and exclusive, the air perfumed with blooming orange and lemon trees. Flowers tumble in bright profusion over garden walls and houses are tucked into groves of trees, up hillsides or cantilevered over deep precipices. There's everything from modest cottages to Spanish mansions to glass boxes stacked like children's blocks. Not every house is luxurious, but the real estate it sits on is gold.

They sweep upward into a world of flickering sunshine and shade. It's hard to believe that people live in such luxury. This must be where movie stars and doctors and lawyers live. The car slows and they come to a stop in front of a ten-foot iron gate. Beyond the gate is a large two-story Mediterranean house painted sunflower yellow with dark green trim. It looks like a painting by van Gogh.

A man with a blond buzz cut and the overblown physique of a bodybuilder opens the gate and closes it after they pass through. A sparkling fountain is the centerpiece of a sweeping circular drive.

Mr. Escobar parks in front of the entrance to the house. He leaves the car running and Buzz Cut slides behind the wheel as soon as he climbs out.

'Give the M.G. a quick once-over, Fritz,' says Rick. 'I'm going out again.'

Fritz nods, his square face expressionless.

Escobar opens Angel's door and she gets out. Fritz pulls the car into a slot in the four-car garage to the left of the house, kills the engine, takes a cloth from his pocket and dusts off a red sports car.

'Fritz isn't very talkative. I wouldn't have more to do with him than necessary. Come, I'll introduce you to Rosalita. She takes care of the house.'

They enter a tiled foyer. Tropical plants in giant urns flank the steps leading to the sunken living room. A bank of windows opens onto a broad vista spanning a plunging canyon behind the house. There's a statue of St. Francis in a recessed alcove to the right of the door and to the left a holy water font. The ceilings are high and beamed and there's an Old World feeling about the place.

'Ah, here's Rosalita,' he says.

Escobar's housekeeper is a beautiful Mexican girl with long, black hair and luminous, black eyes. She's slender and statuesque and a few years older than Angel. Her full red skirt brushes the tops of her moccasins and heavy turquoise jewelry adorns her ears, wrists and fingers.

'Rosalita, this is Miss Jensen. See to it she has everything she needs including an ice bag for her face. You can put her in Julia's room and give her the guided tour when she's ready. Any questions?'

'No, Señor Escobar,' she says.

'I may be home late, so don't plan dinner around me.' So businesslike all of a sudden. So dismissive. Does he assume she's spending the night? She turns to speak to him, but he's already out the door.

★   ★   ★

Fritz opens the gate. Escobar swings the red convertible onto Eagle Crest and heads down the hill. The sun is warm on

67

his face, the wind ruffling his hair. He isn't sure what to make of the girl. Every time she opens her mouth an evasion or half-truth comes out. If Angel had an uncle, he didn't amount to much. Her clothes are cheap, strictly off the rack. And twenty-one? Maybe in another four or five years.

Putting all that aside, the moment she walked into the restaurant he saw beyond the black eye and the ripped coat. She is a ripe peach whose delicate skin has never been bitten into . . . or so he thinks. If she were anything less, she wouldn't fit into his plan.

5

Missing

Tuesday morning. 9:00 a.m. Hank patches a call through from Tunney.

'Jim, what's up?'

I ease my legs over the edge of the bed, finger-comb my hair. I fumble for my cigarettes, light my first smoke of the day and watch the rain surf past the window.

'You ready for your first case?' says Tunney.

'Sure, whatcha got?'

'A missing person. The Chief needs you to get right on it.'

'You make it sound urgent. How urgent can a cold case be?'

'It's not exactly cold. The girl is eighteen-year-old Louise Crowley. Her father came in this morning. He hasn't seen her since Saturday.'

'I'll take it, but why me?'

'We're tied up with a dead Mexican

— showed up behind the auction barn where there was a big cockfight last night. The boys who aren't working the case are suddenly absorbed in heretofore delinquent paperwork.'

'You want to tell me what's going on?'

'The Crowleys live in the encampment on the other side of the river. Nobody wants anything to do with the Hooverville people. It's not like they're residents . . . exactly. We put up signs on both ends of town for crissake. NO JOBS HERE. KEEP GOING. But, they keep coming like army ants. Texas. Oklahoma. Kansas. Hell, we can't even take care of our own.'

'So, why didn't he?'

'Why didn't he what?'

'Keep going.'

'Oh, that. This is where his car gave out. Broken axel.'

'Can't argue with that, Jim. It's not like he got stranded just to aggravate the good people of Santa Paulina. What's the father's name?'

'Let me see. I wrote it down somewhere. Here it is. Walter. Walter Crowley.'

'Where is he now?'

'We sent him back to the encampment, said an officer would be out to take a report as soon as someone is free. It's a mud hole out there. No one plans on being free until the rains stop.'

'When do the rains stop?'

'Sometime in late April, maybe May.'

That's not exactly what I meant, but I let it pass.

'What's he like, so I know what I'm walking into?'

'Thirty-eight. Looks older. There's not enough fat on his bones to grease a frying pan. Married. Five kids. One missing. Wary of authority.'

'Hmm, wonder why that is?'

'I called you didn't I? It's not like I'm sweeping it under the rug. And watch your back. All those Okies are armed to the hilt.'

'I need an hour to shave and get my caffeine level up to speed.'

'Take your time, big guy. You got wheels yet?'

'Not yet, but it's on the top of my list.'

'The Chief's got that covered. Come down to the station so we can do the paperwork and make it official. You want one of the boys to pick you up?'

'No, I'll grab a taxi out front.'

I run the plan by Hank and he tells me to go for it. A missing kid is a missing kid, he says.

★　★　★

It's a quiet morning at the station. Jim introduces me to the boys. I remember Duggan and Boyle from Saturday night. Boyle returned to the scene the next morning and found the keys to the Caddy in the bushes. Chief Garvey slaps them in my hand and tells me it's mine to drive for getting the riffraff off the streets. I'd tell him the credit goes to Angel but why complicate a good thing. I want to keep her name out of it and I want the car.

The Chief is a solid good-looking man in his fifties with snow-white hair and denim blue eyes. He's that curious Irish mix of backslapping affability and thinly disguised menace — the kind of man who's a good drinking buddy, but someone you don't want to cross. He'd find no contradiction in going to Mass on Sunday and beating a confession out of some poor slob on Monday. I'd smell whiskey on his breath if I hadn't washed down my morning pain pills with Teague's brandy. I leave the station thinking I'll probably fit in if I don't play the big-city-cop card.

The car floats like a dream down Cork St. toward the river . . . 'float' being the operative word. The car is shiny and clean with classy leather seats. Nothing but quality for Teague. If I want to get as rich as a pimp I'm working the wrong side of the badge. He was a thorn in my side, but I get the last laugh. I'm driving his car and drinking his brandy. I also ended up with his girl . . . for five minutes.

Wind pummels the car, the wipers slapping away the rain in arching sheets. I think about the Hooverville and what it's like living there on a day like today, or any day for that matter. Rain. Cold. Mud. Lack of electricity and sanitary facilities.

I cross the bridge over the Santa Paulina. The water has risen another six feet since Saturday night. Even with the car windows closed I can hear the roar. I make a right into the dirt road that runs between the woods and the berm. It doesn't have an official name but Jim says everyone calls it River Road. It might be dirt in summer. Now it's a sloppy mire.

I think about the classy car and how dirty it's going to get. I think about my city shoes and how I'll get cowboy boots like the other guys on the Force. I no longer think of them as an affectation. They're durable and they look a hell of a lot more sexy caked with mud than the dress shoes I have on. Today I feel like the city mouse on his cousin's pig farm.

The encampment is in a grove of button willows a half-mile in from the bridge. Moldering in the rain is a cluster of twenty or so shanties comprised of plywood, tarpaper and corrugated metal, similar to the forts I constructed in vacant lots when I was a kid. There are a few war surplus tents and shabby trailers. Vehicles, both operable and unsalvageable, sit up to their hubcaps in muck. Trash cans overflow with refuse and rainwater and broken furniture, and old tires are scattered around with no place to haul them and nothing to haul them in. It is not a pleasant day in Hooverville.

I park in the road for fear of getting capsized in the mud along the shoulder. Doesn't look like anyone's coming in or out anyway. By the time I turn off the wipers and kill the engine, a man has appeared in the doorway of one of the shanties. There's a car with a broken axel off to the side and a coil of smoke rising from a metal pipe sticking out of the roof. He fits the description of Crowley. I raise a hand and he acknowledges me with a nod.

I duck into the collar of my trench coat and tread a line of loose boards leading to the door. They're slippery beneath the slick, hard soles of my shoes.

'Mr. Crowley?' I say as I approach.

'Yes sir, Walter Crowley.'

'I'm Jack Dunning with the Santa Paulina Police Department.'

I extend my hand and we shake. His hand is hard and sinewy like the rest of him. There's not much to him, but what's there has the potential of an un-sprung wolf trap. Rain pours off the low roof of the shack and the branches of the willows overhead. He invites me inside. We duck down and pass through a low door that hangs by leather hinges.

It's warm inside. A pot of coffee perks next to a Dutch oven of beans simmering on the top of a woodstove made from a five-gallon drum. There's a lazy leak in the roof in the right rear of the room. A full-size mattress sits on a tarp against the left wall. I recognize the flowered bedspread as having come from Dobie Gunderson's room at The Rexford. Several small rugs cover the dirt floor and crumpled newspaper is bunched in the cracks of the walls to keep out the drafts.

'Can I pour you a cup of coffee?' he asks.

'No thanks, I'm fine.'

Walter offers me a seat on a five-gallon bucket and we sit across from one another, his seat the same as mine. A mixed collie gets up from behind the stove, walks over and lays his head on Crowley's knee. He whines softly and looks imploringly into the man's eyes. He has thick blond fur with white chest and boots, the kind of dog every child who reads Albert Peyson Terhune wants for a companion. He ruffles the dog's ears.

Crowley looks more like fifty-eight than thirty-eight. His skin is badly weathered with a couple of suspicious black spots near his right temple. He's slightly stooped, like most men who've had lives of hard labor. His green eyes, however, are alert and intelligent. He pats the dog on the head.

'Go lay down, Danny,' he says, and the dog goes back behind the stove and plunks down on a blanket with a labored groan. 'The old boy hasn't been the same since Louise . . . well . . . since we don't know where she is.'

'That's why I'm here, Mr. Crowley. I want to help you find Louise. First, if you don't mind I'd like to get the lay of the land. I understand you have four children, not counting your missing daughter.'

'Yes, they're all younger than Louise. I sent them next door so our conversation

77

doesn't upset them.'

'That was the right thing to do. I imagine you've already spoken with them.'

'I have, and I don't see as they have anything to offer.'

I take a pen and pad out of my inside coat pocket

'Where's Mrs. Crowley?'

'Hazel works up at the big house.' He says it like a southerner . . . the big house . . . the manor . . . the white house on the hill.

'When you say 'big house', what house are you referring to?'

'That would be Romney Kingsolver's place. Owns a section of apples down the main highway.'

'You mean the road to Stockton?'

'That's the one. He's a widow-man, needs someone to do for him — laundry, windows, floors, that kind of thing. Hazel's never been afraid of hard work.'

'What are her hours?'

'Irregular. She never knows from one day to the next. It's just whenever he needs her services.'

'And how does she get there?'

'If he can't pick her up at the crossroads, she hitches — walks if she has to — but I'm sure someone would pick her up in bad weather. I'd drive her myself but you can see the shape my car's in.'

'You say you last saw Louise on Saturday.'

'Yes, Saturday afternoon. I went to empty the slop jar down by the river. She was reading to the kids when I left and when I returned she was gone.'

'Any idea where she might go?'

'I thought she was probably visiting a couple doors down with her friend Eleanor Kapp, but Eleanor hasn't seen her either.'

'Which place is Eleanor's?'

'The army tent three doors down. There's two old tires to the right of the flap.'

'Can you think of any reason Louise might decide to leave voluntarily?' I'm thinking about the bed, wondering how it could accommodate the number of people in the Crowley household. Maybe

79

she felt squeezed out. He shook his head.

'I hope you understand that if I find Louise and she's left voluntarily, I can't force her to return. At eighteen she's no longer a minor.'

'If she left of her own free will she'd have to have money. As far as I can see she was wearing the clothes on her back and nothing else.'

'No purse missing? No suitcase unaccounted for?'

'No. Like I said, just the clothes on her back.'

'Does she have problems with anyone in the encampment? Any arguments? Any enemies?'

'Not Louise. She gets on with everyone. Just ask around. I can't think of anyone would have a bad word to say about her.'

'How about boyfriends?'

'She was seeing a lot of the Galadette boy, Thad, but Hazel and I put a stop to it.'

'Is there something objectionable about the boy, or is it boys in general you don't want her to associate with?'

'Girls get this age, you want to keep them close to home. We don't need complications. You know, boy-girl stuff.'

'I mean no offense, sir, but is there any possibility that Louise is in a family way and afraid to tell you?'

I figure he is going to answer me or shoot me. The shotgun leaning against the back wall did not go unnoticed.

'We haven't seen any indications.'

Crowley seems an honest, decent man, concerned about his family, down on his luck.

'And the Galadette boy. Any violent tendencies?'

'Haven't seen any indication of that either.' He scratches his ear. 'I can't imagine anywhere she'd want to go in the pouring rain.'

I assure Mr. Crowley I'll do everything I can to recover his daughter. He provides me with a slightly dated photo of Louise. She's an attractive girl with long brown hair and her father's intelligent green eyes.

'Where are you from, Mr. Crowley? What did you do before you came west?'

'We're from outside Dalhart, Texas. We did the same as everyone else. Grew wheat until the drought. You've had more rain in two days than we've had in three years. My pa got two dollars a bushel during the Great War. We did good back then, built houses, bought cars and farm equipment. Then the world turned to dust and the wind blew away everything but the mortgage.'

6

Night Whispers

Angel has a big room to herself. There's a bed with a regal hand-carved headboard and an adjoining bathroom. The drawers, dressing table and walk-in closet hold everything a girl could need. There's a charming window seat that overlooks the circular driveway and the gates beyond.

Angel has never known this kind of affluence, although her family lived well in Banning where her father was a mining engineer for a drilling company. They had a modern house with all the amenities, plenty of books and an upright piano. She liked school and got good grades. Then came Teague and her childhood was forever gone. You can reclaim some things that are stolen from you, but your childhood isn't one of them.

After a long, hot shower and a nap,

Angel goes through the clothes in the closet . . . all so new . . . all so expensive. Why would any girl, no matter how wealthy, abandon these beautiful things unless she was very spoiled? How odd that the sizes run from seven to twelve. That would indicate a dramatic weight fluctuation in a short period of time. Angel puts on a pair of tan slacks and a white, long-sleeved blouse to cover the bite on her arm, which is now red with inflammation.

Rosalita knocks on the door and peeks into the room. 'Did the ice bag help?'

'Yes, thank you so much, Rosalita. I didn't mean to sleep so long.'

'Soon I will be starting dinner. There is a choice of steak, lobster, game hens or . . . '

'What are you having?'

'Enchiladas, Spanish rice, and beans.'

'I'll have the same. Would you like some help in the kitchen?'

'No thank you. This is all very easy to do.'

'In that case I'm going to explore the grounds.'

'After dinner I will take you on a tour of the house.'

Angel slips leather sandals on her feet and skips down the staircase, her shoes slapping softly against the tiles. She pushes through the heavy door and takes a deep breath of flower-scented air. No rain. No cold. Just glorious sunshine. When she closes her eyes she pretends it's her mother's hand on her cheek. She sits on the edge of the fountain and runs her fingers through the water.

At the base of the thick stucco walls that enclose the property is a vicious forest of cacti that would deter the boldest fence-jumper. Hummingbirds flicker like jewels among the flowerbeds that line the circular drive. It's quiet and restful, just the splash of the fountain and the distant hum of traffic from the city below.

Angel strolls to the front gate. A chain holds the sections in place. The embankment across the street is thick with eucalyptus, scrub oak, and wild grass. She wonders who the neighbors are, what their houses look like, if they're famous.

She gives the gates a rattle.

A shadow falls over her shoulder and Fritz materializes at her side.

'You startled me,' she says.

'You startle easily.' He wears a deadpan expression and speaks in a rumbling monotone.

'You walk very quietly for a big man.'

'The gate is locked,' he says.

'Thank you, I noticed that. I'd like to take a walk.'

'There's been a break-in two doors down. I've been told to tighten security.'

'Who told you that?'

'L.A.P.D. Tomorrow you may wander at will,' he says.

'I hadn't planned on being here tomorrow.'

His face is expressionless. He says nothing.

'Where has Mr. Escobar gone?'

'It's not my job to ask questions.'

'What does he do for a living?'

'You should ask him.'

'Thank you, Fritz. You've been most helpful.' She resists the urge to roll her eyes as she walks away. That was certainly a strange conversation.

Angel and Rosalita eat dinner in the dining room. The Mexican girl has changed into a white dress, silver bracelets, earrings, and turquoise rings shining on her fingers. A picture window captures the sun setting in vivid streaks of shocking pink and orange and purple. In the distance, through a break in the hills, is a patch of bright blue ocean.

'Your jewelry is beautiful,' says Angel.

'Thank you, it's been passed down through the family.'

They eat slowly, savoring the spicy food and topping off the meal with fruit and coffee. Angel tries to draw Rosalita into conversation, but the girl says little and only when spoken to. Angel doesn't want to reveal much either, especially about her time with Teague and her life at The Blue Rose Dance Hall. By the time they finish eating, the sky is dark and the city below is sparkling with lights.

'Rosalita, I've never had a more satisfying meal. You're an excellent cook.'

'Thank you, Señorita Jensen.'

'Can't we make that Angel? It would be

so much easier, don't you think?'

'Señor Escobar would never allow it.' Angel reaches across the table and touches her hand. It's tense and cold. She looks like she's carrying the weight of the world.

'Señor Escobar isn't here. It's just you and me.' That gets a hint of a smile. Rosalita's long silver earrings catch the light.

'That's better.'

'Come with me, Angel. I will show you the rest of the house.'

In a large house of hard surfaces, every sound, every footstep, every spoken word is amplified. Even the ticking of the clock has an echo. They traverse a dozen rooms . . . butler's pantry, den, library, music room, conservatory, chapel and four nicely-appointed guest rooms. There's hardly a wall or alcove in the house that doesn't display a framed religious icon or the statue of a saint. It's a large house for one person and a servant.

Rosalita opens the door to Mr. Escobar's room. The colorful bedspread has been turned down on the over-sized bed, a snifter of brandy on the nightstand. There's a Navajo rug on the floor and a collection of medieval weapons on the wall. No feminine touches. No family photos. The room feels chillier and more closed off than the rest of the house.

'I don't think I could sleep with all that artillery on the wall,' says Angel.

'I know. I do not like to come here.'

'What happened to Mr. Escobar's wife?'

'He does not speak of her. Perhaps she died long ago.'

'Don't you wonder?'

'Of course, but I was not hired to ask questions.'

How odd. Fritz said essentially the same thing.

'When do you expect him in?' Angel asks.

'Always late. I never know until he arrives.'

'I guess I'm stuck for the night. That wasn't part of my plan.'

'*Si*, just make yourself comfortable. It is too late to make another plan.'

'What does Mr. Escobar do for a living?'

'He owns a hotel downtown. The El Toro. Sometimes, I look through his mail to see what I can find out.'

'Owning a hotel sounds impressive.'

'It's nothing fancy, just a bar and restaurant with rooms above. It's a few blocks east of a big park called Pershing Square.'

'Is that good?'

'It is a bad neighborhood. He says El Toro is on an historical site and he plans to renovate the building, but Fritz says he doesn't see much going on in the way of construction.'

'I've heard that renovations are costly. He must have family money.' The grandfather clock in the hall strikes the hour. A wall clock answers in a distant room.

'Please excuse me. Already I have said too much.' Rosalita turns and walks away, leaving Angel standing alone at the bottom of the staircase.

★　★　★

Angel lies awake in the big bed. The warm Santa Ana wind blows off the desert and a shutter bangs at the back of the house. She's dying for a cigarette and can't remember going this long without one. When she thinks of cigarettes, she thinks of Jack, the room at The Rexford and how the cinders of their Luckys glowed in the darkness.

Does Jack lie awake at night missing her like she misses him? Or, has he written her off as another cheap tart with sticky fingers? She never should have taken Jack's money. She made a mistake getting on the train. She made a mistake taking a ride from Mr. Escobar. She can't say why, it's just that something about this place doesn't feel right. Jack would have worked things out one way or another, especially if Jim Tunney saw things their way.

2:00 a.m. Car lights sweep the walls of her room. She gets out of bed and sits by the window in the dark. Escobar climbs out of the sports car and unlocks the gate. He drives onto the property and locks the chain in place behind him. She wonders what his business was at the railway station and wishes she had asked more questions.

He parks in an empty space in the garage and walks to the front of the house. The door opens and closes. He comes up the stairs, pauses, then walks past her room to his bedroom at the far end of the hall. She hears the shower running and after a brief interval his door opens a second time. His footsteps come back down the hall toward her room.

Angel moves silently to the door and depresses the button in the center of the knob. Footsteps stop outside her room. In the crack beneath the door she sees a shadow backlit by the hall light. A hand, ever so tentatively, tries the knob.

'Angel? Are you awake?' A whisper. He waits for a response. After a few seconds he continues down the hall. Angel leans with her back against the door, barely breathing. Without knocking he enters Rosalita's room.

'Get up, Rosie. You need to turn down my bed and join me in a drink.'

'I have already turned down your bed, Señor.'

'Then you must do it again, the right way this time.'

'I am tired. It has been a long day.'

'Are you refusing me?' There's an edge to his voice. He's no longer the conciliatory gentleman who took a punch trying to retrieve her purse.

'I am coming, Señor Escobar.'

Angel climbs back in bed and pulls the covers over her head.

★ ★ ★

At five-thirty Rosalita returns to her room and runs the shower. At six she goes downstairs. Angel follows a few minutes later.

Mr. Escobar is sitting at the table with coffee and orange juice, reading the business section of the morning paper. He looks up and smiles his matinee idol smile. He's wearing the kind of breezy white suit rich men wear in the tropics.

'Good morning, Angel. I hope the wind didn't keep you up.'

'No, I slept well, thank you.'

'Sit down. Breakfast will be ready in a minute.'

A dish shatters in the kitchen, then the sound of broken glass being swept into a wastebasket.

'Oh dear, these tile floors are murder on the dishware. Then again, Rosie isn't the most graceful of girls,' he says with a wink.

Angel feels sick to her stomach. She was graceful enough to drag herself to your bed last night. She bites her tongue for fear of saying it out loud.

'I'm going job hunting this morning,' she says. 'If I'm still allowed an outfit or two, I'll pay you out of my first paycheck.'

He looks surprised, perhaps a bit offended.

'Has Rosie made you feel unwelcome here?'

'She's been very good to me, but the sooner I'm on my own the better.'

'I find that commendable. Speaking of employment, do you type?'

'I took typing in school. I'm neither a racehorse nor a snail, but I'm accurate.'

Angel seems different today, more centered, as if she's had time to process the unsettling events of the day before.

'Give me a day or two. I know an accountant who's looking for a secretary. No sense pounding the pavement unless you have to.' Rosalita enters the room and lays out a breakfast of scrambled eggs and toast. 'Perfect, as always,' he says, giving her a look that makes Angel cringe. Rosalita gives her a glance, much like the waitress at the restaurant had.

'Fritz seems to be obsessed with locks and chains,' says Angel. 'It makes me uncomfortable.'

'He's far too security-conscious at times. I'll have a word with him.' He pulls a money clip from his pocket, peels off a twenty and sets it next to Angel's saucer. 'In case you want to do a little shopping on the boulevard, Fritz can drive you.'

After he leaves, Angel goes to the kitchen. Rosalita sits quietly in the breakfast nook with her cup of coffee. Angel slides into the seat across from her. Rosalita's mouth is raw with whisker burn, her eyes red from crying. Angel touches her hand.

'Don't look at me,' she says, pulling her hand away and covering her face.

'I know what happened last night. It wasn't your fault. Why don't you leave?'

'I can't.'

'Why? Help me understand what's going on here.'

'You wouldn't understand.'

'Maybe I would.'

Angel rolls up the sleeve of her blouse, exposing the angry bite on her arm.

'Señor Escobar did that?'

'No, but someone like him did. What is he holding over your head?'

'If I tell you, it will only make things worse.'

'I doubt that.'

'My baby has been stolen. My little boy, Matías. Señor Escobar is my only hope to get him back.'

'How long ago did this happen?'

'Two weeks ago.'

'How long have you been here?'

'Since the night he was stolen from my arms.'

'Have you gone to the police?'

'That I cannot do. I am here illegally. Señor Escobar says that if the police find out, they will send me back to Mexico and I will never get my son back.'

* * *

Escobar knocks on Fritz's apartment door at the rear of the garage. Fritz lowers his weights to the concrete floor with a metallic clatter.

'Angel expects you to drive her into town today,' said Escobar, pulling on his pigskin driving gloves.

'So?'

'Too bad your Chevy's on the blink.'

'What are you talking about? There's nothing wrong with . . . '

'Don't be so dense.'

'Okay, I get it Boss. You don't have to beat me over the head.'

'Sometimes I wonder. You get any ideas about that girl and . . . '

'That's your game, not mine,' says Fritz, unconsciously flexing a fist.

Escobar shoots him a dangerous look.

Fritz rolls the tension from his

shoulders and jogs to the gate, arms and thighs bulging with muscle. He unlocks the chain and swings the gate wide as the red car blows past, missing him by inches.

'You don't know who you're dealing with,' says Fritz to himself, as he watches the red car disappear down the hill.

7

Digging Deeper

I step outside of the Crowleys' shack. The rain has let up and the temperature plunges. I stand beneath the dripping trees and take a closer look at the two-year-old photo of missing Louise Crowley. Her father says she still wears her brown hair long, sometimes in braids and sometimes flowing down her back. He can't remember how she wore it the last day he saw her, but says she's changed little since the photo was taken. She's taller, about five seven, her freckles are fading and her frame has grown lean and hard. Her weight is a matter of speculation since they have no scale and she hasn't seen a doctor in three years.

I look down the row of rough-and-tumble dwellings and walk to the tent with the tires off to the side. Maybe Eleanor Kapp can throw some light on

99

the mystery of Louise's disappearance. If Louise talked to anyone about problems it would likely be her mother or her best friend. I walk through the slop of mud to the tent as the flap opens and a teenage girl steps outside carrying an empty gunnysack.

'Eleanor Kapp?' I ask.

'What of it?' she says, but it comes out sounding like, you wanna fight?

The girl is sturdy and thick-bodied with a round wind-burned face. She wears an over-sized pea coat and men's boots. A tangle of beige frizz pokes from beneath her wool scarf.

'I'm Officer Dunning.'

'Don't mean nothin' to me unless you found Louise.'

'I hope you can help me with that, Eleanor.'

'I don't see how.'

'You can start by telling me when you saw her last and under what circumstances.'

'That would have been Saturday morning. We went to the river to fill our pails.'

'And after that?'

'There was no after that. It was raining cats and dogs. I went back to the tent and she went back inside her crate.'

'Her crate?'

'Ya, her shack's mostly made of shipping crates.'

'And you're sure that's the last time you saw her?'

'I'm sure. There's nothing wrong with my memory.'

My eyes keep drifting to the deep woods on the far side of the road.

'You think she'd go into the woods?'

'I can't imagine why. The weather was terrible and there's poison oak all over the place.'

'It didn't stop you two from going to the river.'

'We have to go to the river if we want water for cooking.'

'I'm thinking about getting bloodhounds out here.'

'Won't help. The rain woulda washed away the scent by now.'

'You may be right.'

'I am right.'

'How did you and Louise get along?'

'We been best friends since grammar school.'

'Ever argue?'

'Nothing to argue about.'

'Does she have any enemies?'

'Louise? She's not the type. She'd let people walk all over her before she'd say boo.'

'How did she get along at home?'

'You call that dump home?'

'I mean with her parents.'

'Okay, far as I know. Her dad's a quiet sort and her mom ain't there a lot.'

'I guess her mom supports the family.'

'You better not let her old man hear you say that. He's a prideful person.'

'How about boyfriends? Louise seeing anybody?'

'Her parents would go through the roof. They'd never allow it.'

'When I was a kid, I didn't do everything my parents said. How about you, Eleanor?'

She stares at me with a blank look. Beneath the wind-burn her face is pasty and slack, like she has tired blood.

'Are you all right?'

'Do I look all right? Is anyone in this hellhole all right? If I had a dime in my pocket I'd be hitching a ride anyplace but here.'

'You think that's what Louise did? Hitch down the road?'

'She woulda tooken me with her. She knows how much I hate it here.'

'Any particular place you think I should look for Louise, Miss Kapp?'

'You're the cop. You figure it out.'

'Are your parents in?'

'In? Sure. They're at The Do Drop Inn down on Shannon. I gotta go. They told me to collect bottles along the road if the rain stops. It's stopped.'

'How old are you?'

'I just turned seventeen.'

'If you want to wait around until I'm through here, I'll drive you to the main road.'

'I shouldn't even be talking to you.'

Strange kid. She walks away, dragging the weight of the world in her gunnysack.

'One more thing, Eleanor.' She turns back to face me, looking bored and irritable.

'What now?'

'What was Louise's relationship with Thad Galadette?'

'I don't think he was that interested in her.'

'When did Louise first tell you she was pregnant?'

Eleanor's face flushes a bright red. She opens her mouth but nothing comes out.

'Eleanor, what aren't you telling me?'

'Just find Louise. She's the only friend I have in this godforsaken dump.'

I watch her step from the road onto the berm where the winter grass makes for easier walking. She's hard-shelled and over-loaded with life's disappointments. Beneath the crust of neglect I see a girl who might have grown up happy and playful if someone cared enough to run a comb through her hair.

I walk further down the row of dwellings until I see a man collecting firewood from beneath an oilcloth tarp. By now I've given up trying to avoid the mud. It's like going swimming and expecting not to get wet. My socks are wet. My feet are numb with cold. The man turns to face me, his arms loaded down with logs. Everyone else in the encampment is hunkered inside trying to keep warm.

'What can I do you for?' he says. He's bundled in a red plaid jacket and matching cap with ear flaps. He has symmetrical features, blond hair and a sturdy build that's beginning to run to fat.

'I'm Jack Dunning. Chief Garvey sent me to investigate the disappearance of Louise Crowley. You know her?'

'Sure, I know who she is. I'm Grady Galadette. I'd shake if my arms weren't full. I heard the girl hasn't been seen in a couple days.'

'Any theories?'

'Same as everybody else's.'

'What are everybody else's?'

'That she run off. She's eighteen now. When I was eighteen, me and my buddies got jobs and run off, too. Wanted our independence. Didn't want our parents telling us what we could and couldn't do. 'As long as you live under my roof you do what I say or get out.' Isn't a kid in the world hasn't heard that one a million times. I've said it myself on occasion.'

'Those were different times, Mr. Galadette. First of all, if you've read the signs for the last hundred miles, you'd know that there aren't any jobs, and the ones that did exist were grabbed up by men who have families to support like yourself. Isn't a young girl out there has a chance of making it on her own.'

'Who says she's on her own?'

'You know something I don't?'

Galadette gives a deprecating shrug.

'It's just that Walter's little filly is hot to trot.'

'That's a pretty strong statement, Mr. Galadette. Would you care to elaborate?'

'She hung around bothering my son until I put a stop to it.'

'You or Mr. Crowley?'

'Both of us, I guess. It's common knowledge that Louise was a little too generous with her affections. I have hopes for my son that don't include a shotgun wedding.'

'I'm sure no parent wants that, Mr.

Galadette. When did you last see Louise?'
The wood had become heavy in his arms.
He let it fall to the ground to show his
annoyance at being questioned on so
trivial a matter as the disappearance of a
young girl he didn't like.

'At least a week ago.'

'Was she alone?

'She was going into the tent with
Eleanor what's-her-name.'

'Kapp?'

'Right. That's the last time I seen her.'

'When did your son last see Louise?'

'A month ago. That's when Crowley
told her to stop bothering him.'

'How bothered was your son, Mr.
Galadette?'

A vein throbbed in Galadette's forehead. Temper, temper, Mr. Galadette.

'He didn't have a say in the matter. I
was bothered. My wife, Johanna, was
bothered. She's confined to a wheelchair
and I don't want her upset. That boy is
the apple of her eye.'

'I'm sure the Crowleys have similar
sentiments regarding their daughter.'

Behind Galadette is a cabin built onto

the bed of a flatbed truck. It's well-constructed, white with red trim, a fancy rooster weathervane sticking up from the roof. A thin spiral of smoke leaks from the chimney pipe.

'You build that?' I ask.

'Yes, before we left Oklahoma.'

'Looks comfortable.'

'I plan ahead.' The vein settles down. He'd rather talk about cabins than his son and the missing girl. 'My father was a master carpenter. I picked up a thing or two along the way.'

'It's nice to be high and dry. Does the truck run?'

'It will when I put a new battery in it.'

'You're in no big rush to be out of here, are you, Mr. Galadette?'

'Not in particular.' A tic fires off at the corner of his eye.

'That's good.'

He rubs sweat from his forehead with the back of his hand.

'Are you accusing me of something?'

'Is Thad in?'

He can see where this conversation is headed.

'What do you want with my son?

'His name surfaced a few times in my investigation,' I say.

'This is bullshit.'

'I guess bullshit is part of my job. If you feel you're being treated unfairly, you can file a complaint with the Chief.'

He takes his cap off, runs his fingers through his hair, puts it back on again.

'It's just that the cops treat us like criminals down here, always wanting to pin something on us to clear their cases. Better us than some local, right?'

'It's not that complicated, Mr. Galadette. I'm just trying to locate a missing girl. I appreciate any cooperation I can get.'

'Thad's inside. Why don't you come on in?'

'I'd prefer it if he'd step out. I'd like to speak to him in private.'

He's about to protest, then thinks better of it. He turns without a word, climbs the cinder block steps that lead to the bed of the truck and disappears inside the cabin, leaving the logs scattered around my feet.

★ ★ ★

The young man steps out in the time it takes to put on his coat and get a little coaching from dad. Thad is a strapping younger version of his father, same good features, same nice coat except his is blue instead of red. He wears his blond curls longer than most fellows but it suits him.

'I'm Thad,' he says, extending his hand. His grip is firm but non-aggressive.

'I'm Jack Dunning. I'm sure your father has already told you why I'm here.'

'Yes, I'm glad that someone in authority is finally on the job.' He glances over his shoulder. A shadow moves behind the curtain in the cabin window. 'You mind if we walk?' he says.

'Why don't we talk in the car and get out of the wind.'

We walk back past the Kapps and the Crowleys and sit in the front seat of the Caddy.

'I've seen this car before,' he says. 'It belonged to that gangster got shot the other night.'

'Where he's going he won't need it anymore.'

The kid smiles. He has a nice smile and good teeth. 'I guess that's true.'

'Why don't you tell me about Louise?'

'All I know is that no matter what my dad says she hasn't run off.'

'How can you be so sure?'

'Because we were planning to run off together. Please don't tell my dad. He'd kill me if he knew.'

'That's a pretty drastic decision given how rough things are out there.'

'Things are rough here too. If everybody wasn't trying to keep us apart we might have decided to stay, but we can't reason with Mr. Crowley and we certainly can't reason with my dad.'

'Yes, he left me with that impression. Not the most flexible fellow I've ever met.'

'Just try living with him.'

'If Louise hasn't run off, what do you think has happened to her?'

'Something bad. I was searching the woods this morning. I could swear someone took a potshot at me, but I never saw who.'

'Why would she go into the woods in the pouring rain?'

'I don't know, but she has no money and no car and I couldn't come up with a better idea.'

'Was she receiving unwanted advances from anyone, maybe someone who wanted to catch her alone?'

'She would have said something to me. I'm sure of it.'

'Had you argued? Is there a rival for her affections? Does she have enemies?'

'None of the above. That's why it's so confusing. It's like she went up in smoke.'

'Who else knew about your plan to run off?'

'I didn't tell anybody.'

'Would Louise have told someone?'

'If she had, it probably would have been Eleanor.'

'I just spoke with her, but she's not very forthcoming. How would she have felt about you two going off together?'

'Who knows? I don't know why Louise bothers with her. Miss gloom and doom. She hates everybody, loves to wallow in her own misery. Things are dismal enough without someone dragging you down. Once I took her to the movies just because I felt sorry for her, but no matter what you do to cheer her up, it's never enough.'

'I see why Louise might want to leave home because of the crowded conditions, but you seem to have things better than most folks around here ... nice clothes ... good cabin.'

'You don't know what it's like living with my dad. He has to control everything — who my friends are, where I go, when I get up, when I go to bed. I'll be nineteen next month for golly sake and he's still beating me with the belt. He calls it the Bible belt. Spare the rod and all that baloney. It's the only verse he's memorized in the whole book.'

'That's got to be tough.'

'It is. I could punch his lights out sometimes, but I'd rather leave before it comes to that.'

'I can see that you and Louise are very close. Is there any chance that she might be pregnant?'

113

'None at all. We've never gone that far. In fact . . . '

He blushes and looks out the passenger side window.

'You were about to say?'

'It's a little embarrassing. When I met Louise I thought I could get a girl pregnant by kissing her. It's what my mother always told me. Louise couldn't believe my folks never filled me in on the birds and bees. She could have made fun of me, but she didn't.'

'She sounds like a nice girl.'

He turns toward me and looks me straight in the eye. 'She's the best, Officer Dunning. The very best. You've got to find her.'

'I certainly hope to. It's the only thing on my plate right now. Won't you two need money to make your great escape?'

'Sure. I almost have enough.'

'You work?'

He pulls a small wooden angel from his pocket and puts it in my hand. She's kneeling with her eyes closed, her expression peaceful. I can see every delicately carved feather on the folded wings. I'm flooded with thoughts of Angel Doll.

'You all right, Officer?'

'Yes Thad. Your work is amazing.'

'Thank you. I've been carving ever since I was a little boy.'

'I wonder if you know how good you are.'

'Thank you for saying that. My dad says it's sissy stuff. I like to carve angels. I also sell different kinds of crosses outside the Baptist Church. I carve roses into the wood. The ladies like them.'

'I bet they do. What do you ask for something like this?'

'I get fifty cents on a good day, but I'm willing to take what I can get.'

'Would you sell it to me?'

'Sure. Some people think angels bring good luck.'

Thad walks back to his cabin, four bits richer. I set the angel on the dash and think of the skill it takes to create something this intricate. I light a cigarette, which is the extent of my own manual dexterity. It doesn't take long to smoke up the cab and for the soothing chemicals to untie the knots at the back of my neck. I wish it could help me untie the knots in the Louise Crowley case.

I update my notes while everything is fresh in my mind. Have I learned anything of value from today's interviews? Walter Crowley wants his daughter home or he wouldn't have walked to the police station and back in the pouring rain to file a missing persons report. I make a note to speak with Hazel Crowley. She may be privy to information her husband isn't keyed into.

Eleanor Kapp is an enigma. She certainly knows more than she's willing to divulge. She knows that Louise and Thad continued to see one another after their parents forbade it. If Louise wasn't pregnant, why did Eleanor react the way she had? She probably knew of Louise's plan to run off with Thad. Was she supportive or resentful that Thad is going off with her only close friend? Is she capable of being happy for someone else, or is she too steeped in her own misery? What was it Thad had said? 'No matter what you do to cheer her up, it's never enough.'

Grady Galadette. He's defensive about something, maybe everything. Is he responsible for Louise's disappearance? He has a motive. She set her cap for his blond-haired boy, the apple of his invalid mother's eye. He's made it clear that there better not be any shotgun weddings in the Galadette family. He did his best to keep me from talking with Thad outside of his presence. What was that about? Was he being the over-protective father, or does he believe that Thad is involved in Louise's disappearance? Then again, he might fear his son will reveal something about him, something more damning than beating his boy with a belt.

Once I've raised my nicotine intake to a tolerable level, I spend another hour questioning people at the encampment. I don't learn anything new. My initial impression is that Thad has no involvement in Louise's disappearance. That doesn't mean I haven't been fooled in the past and that I couldn't be fooled again. He says that Louise couldn't be pregnant because they'd never gone that far. That doesn't mean that she hasn't gone that far with someone else. She knew a lot more about the birds and bees than he did. And what about Thad's account of being fired at in the woods?

I drive slowly back the way I came, the encampment on the river side of the road, the woods on the other. I peer into the thick, wet tangle of foliage, but beyond a few feet all I see is darkness. What reason would Louise have to venture into the cold, wet woods, and why would Thad think of looking for her there?

I pull onto the main road, but instead of driving back toward town I drive along the perimeter of the woods in the opposite direction. I think of the skeletal remains found in thickets and swamps and remote fields, and how isolated areas make for good body dumps. I drive for a mile until the trees yield to agricultural fields and orchards, then turn back toward town.

I go by the offices of the *Morning Sun* with Louise's photo. They agree to run it along with a plea to the public to come forward with information regarding her disappearance or whereabouts.

I report back to the Chief. I smell whiskey on his breath. He's in a good mood, slaps me on the back and tells me to follow the clues wherever they lead. 'I like a lad who's quick out of the gate. We're going to get on just fine,' he tells me.

'Anybody around here have tracking dogs?' I ask.

'Sure, Gil Guffy out on Old Adobe Road.' He writes his phone number on a piece of paper and hands it to me. I make the call from my desk.

'Won't do no good,' says Guffy. 'Too much rain.' What do I know? I'm from Boston. It's not like you see many packs of bloodhounds in Southie. Chalk one up for Eleanor Kapp.

I rinse the mud off of my shoes behind The Rexford — not that they'll ever again look like the ones I put on this morning. I shower and change and check in with Hank, who hands me a few rental applications to go over. After they check out, I do a welfare check on a couple of elderly tenants to make sure they're still alive and kicking. They're simply tucked in with their knitting and crossword puzzles, waiting for spring.

I take a wooden box out of my sock drawer and set it on top of the dresser. Inside are a few sets of cuff links and two pocket watches. One is made of a dull metal that simulates silver. It belonged to my grandfather. The other one has a twenty-four carat gold case. I won it when I fanned out three jacks and two nines in a poker game. It's the kind of thing you don't wear in hard times unless you want to get mugged. I take it down the street to Sal's Pawnshop and trade it for a handsome pair of hand-tooled cowboy boots, two pairs of lightly worn jeans and a hotplate.

I find a photo of Angel Doll amongst her things. I call L.A.P.D. from my room and file a missing persons report. I include the phone number of the station and The Rexford. Then I go to the newspaper office and have them follow up by wiring down the photo.

That night I put the angel on the

nightstand. I drink brandy from a whiskey glass and smoke three cigarettes, lighting the next one off the cinder from the last. I have a job to do. I have two lost girls that need to be found and I'm going to find them both.

8

Secrets and Clues

The cold, wet days drone on. Customers come and go from Madame Zarina's cozy Victorian parlor with its muted lamplight and soft furnishings of velvet. She dispenses advice and encouragement with hugs and sugared tea and collects dimes and nickels in a flowered cup she keeps on a shelf in her china cabinet.

She hasn't stopped thinking about the young lady in the woods and wonders if Officer Swackhammer has passed along her message to Chief Garvey. If only her vision had been more complete. She's left with more questions than answers. Is the young lady dead, or is she still waiting for rescue? Can she survive her wounds, the damp and the cold nights? Has anyone reported her missing? As Cookie drinks her morning coffee, one of her questions is answered.

The photo of Louise Ruth Crowley looks up from the second page of the Santa Paulina *Morning Sun*. She's been reported missing by her father, Walter Crowley, who last saw her Saturday at the Hooverville on River Road. There is no doubt in Cookie's mind that this is the same green-eyed lady in her vision. She finishes her coffee and donuts and goes downstairs to the bakery. The bell jingles as a customer goes out the door with a pink bag of pastries and coffee in a paper cup.

'Joe, look at this,' she says, showing him the picture of the missing girl. He closes the drawer of the cash register and walks over to the counter where she's spread the newspaper.

'Well, I'll be,' he says.

'She's lying out in the woods and nobody knows it. Why do you think the Chief hasn't called?'

'What do you want to bet it's that damn Swackhammer? If his uncle wasn't councilman he couldn't get elected dog catcher. Listen Cookie, you get yourself dolled up and I'll drive you down to the

123

station when I close for lunch. We need to light a fire under that bozo. Whether she's dead or alive, that little girl needs to be back with her family.'

★   ★   ★

Louise can't remember how long she's been here. She tries to move, but a bolt of lightning spears her in the lower back. If her coat was thinner or the blade of the knife had been longer, she would be dead. She's eaten a few mushrooms that tumbled from her basket, but at night her damp hair freezes to the ground. She's not sure she can survive another night in the woods.

All she can think about is Thad, her parents, and her four little brothers. She misses the warm cabin where Dad keeps a pot of beans or a beef stew simmering on the woodstove. They've been through a lot together since they lost the farm and her parents are doing everything they can to keep the family together. Louise tries one more time to roll over, but collapses in pain.

I walk into the station in my cowboy boots and sheepskin jacket. With the passing of the rain, the temperature has plummeted. Jim, the Chief and several other officers are still working the auction barn case, leaving Swack on desk duty and Green typing up a semi-literate report of a deer-poaching incident outside of town. I update my report and put it on the Chief's desk.

Where is Louise Crowley? Has she left voluntarily? Did she fall in the river and drown? If so, she'd be far downstream by now. She may have been walking to the Kingsolver's to see her mother, been hit by a car and left in a ditch. Has she been the victim of foul play?

I consider the possibility of kidnapping or sexual assault, but it's statistically unlikely. This is not the season of bare bodies, honey-dipped tans, wild abandon and raging hormones. It's a time for bundling up in front of a fire and conserving one's energy.

After walking the riverbank two hundred yards in both directions and finding no clues, I spend hours driving the highway and back roads, scanning the tree line, the ditches and the open fields. I trek into the woods and follow overgrown paths until they become impassable. I search old barns and abandoned houses and show Louise's photo, without success, to everyone I see. Late in the day I return to the encampment to check in with Crowley. As soon as I get out of the car he walks over.

'What's going on, Mr. Crowley?'

'I think someone is targeting my family,' he says.

'What's happened?'

'It's my dog, Danny. I let him out to do his business this morning and he never came back.'

'Is that unusual?'

'Yes. He spends most of his time sleeping behind the stove. He's too old to wander and he can't make it as far as the highway because of his arthritis. I think he's been shot or poisoned. First Louise and now Danny. If you ask me, Grady

Galadette is behind this.'

'Why do you think that, Mr. Crowley?'

'First of all, he doesn't think Louise is good enough for his son, and she goes missing. He thinks his family is better than mine and lets us know it. I can't think of anybody else who'd have an ax to grind.'

'I don't see what he'd have to gain by killing your dog.' Then again, I don't think there was much to gain by beating his son with a belt.

'He'd do it out of sheer meanness.'

'I'll have a word with him, Mr. Crowley. I'd suggest you stay away from him. I don't want this thing turning into the Hatfields and the McCoys.'

A commotion erupts down the path. Grady Galadette and Eleanor Kapp are having a heated exchange in front of the flatbed. Thad is nowhere in sight. Grady extends his hands in a placating gesture, but Eleanor is having none of it. He's an unpopular guy this morning. She shouts something in his face, knocks his cap to the ground and stomps off. He bends down and picks it up, sees us watching and goes up the steps to his cabin.

'What the hell is that about?' I say.

'With those two it's hard to tell,' says Crowley. 'She used to have a crush on Thad. You can imagine how Galadette felt about that.'

'When I talked to him, he pretended to barely know who she is.'

'He knows her well enough to argue with,' says Crowley.

Eleanor glares at me as she stomps our way. Her face is red and blotchy with fury, her chunky arms folded across her chest, her body thick and ungainly in her pea coat. She steps into her tent and drops the flap.

'I'll talk to her after she settles down,' I say.

'That girl never settles down.'

'Her parents ever show?'

'No, and they won't as long as there's an empty bar stool to sit on.'

Four little Crowley boys bundled up like Eskimos emerge from the shanty. They're close in age, between three and ten years old, laughing and joking and tussling playfully with each other. They're cute kids, freckled and redheaded.

'You have good-looking boys, Mr. Crowley.' I can see the pride in his face as he looks at his children.

'I try to bring 'em up right.'

'Is Mrs. Crowley home today?'

'No, Hazel stayed on at the Kingsolver's last night. It's easier than finding her way out there again in the morning.'

'Seems sensible,' I say, 'the weather being what it is. I think I'll swing on out and get her perspective on things.'

* * *

'Wouldn't you know that Swackhammer's on duty today,' whispers Cookie to Joe as they walk into the station.

Joe looks dignified in his tweed overcoat and handsome fedora, and Cookie is nicely pulled together in her red wool coat and matching hat. They stand for several seconds in front of Swackhammer's desk as he reads a magazine and pretends not to notice them. Finally, he looks up.

'What can I do for you?' he asks,

shifting a cud of tobacco from one cheek to the other.

'We'd like to speak with Chief Garvey,' says Joe.

'Can't help you. He's out to the auction barn where that guy got shot.'

'Who's in charge of the Louise Crowley case?' says Cookie.

'That would be the new guy, some city slicker out of Boston.'

'Does this city slicker have a name?'

'Dunning. Jack Dunning. He's out working the case as we speak.'

'I never heard back from Chief Garvey,' says Cookie. 'Are you sure you passed on my message?'

'Of course I did. Can't say he put much stock in it though.'

Green gives Swackhammer a disapproving look over the top of his typewriter.

'Well, if Dunning is looking for the Crowley girl in anyplace other than the woods, he won't find her. She's been stabbed and she's lying in the leaves unable to move. I don't think she can last another night in the cold,' says Cookie.

'Stabbed by who?'

'I don't know. She can tell you when you find her. Cookie hands him a carefully written note. 'I want you to give this to the new man or to Chief Garvey, whichever one you see first. It's important if you want to find that girl alive.'

'Your wish is my command, Madame Zarina,' he says, taking possession of the note.

'She's Mrs. Cook to you, Swackhammer,' says Joe. He takes a step closer to the desk and Swack leans back when he sees the look in Joe's eye.

Joe looks over at Officer Green.

'You saw that note, Green,' he says. 'If this goes off track I'll see that both of your heads fly.'

Swack looks out the window and watches Joe's Buick pull away from the curb. He throws his head back and laughs, a dribble of tobacco running down his chin. He crumples up the note.

'What the hell are you doing?' says Green. 'You're going to get us both canned. It ain't funny no more.'

'I don't take orders from them. Why

bother the Chief with this crap?'

'You do it because they ask you to. She reported the girl missing before any of us knew there was a girl. I tell you Swack, there's something to this.'

Above Swack's desk is a ceiling fixture. It looks like a white upside-down fruit bowl hanging from a trio of chains. He crunches the note into a tight ball and shoots it toward the fixture. On the third try it catches precariously on the rim. It doesn't go in and it doesn't come out.

'I'd like to see you top that,' says Swack.

'I bet that kind of thing got a big laugh back in kindergarten,' says Green.

* * *

I turn onto the main highway at the crossroads and drive south. It's late in the day and I'm losing the light. I pass Sparkey's Roadhouse, the parking lot already filling up with cars. I drive another mile before the apple orchard appears along the right-hand side of the road. The acreage rolls away to the west

132

until it bumps against foothills green with winter rain.

Another half-mile and I see the Kingsolver's mailbox. I turn down a long, gravel driveway. There's a big white house and several large apple sheds. I park in front of the house and ease from the car. It's been a long day and my back is giving out. I limp up the steps of a veranda hung with baskets of plants that have succumbed to the cold.

A plump middle-aged woman opens the door to my knock. She wipes flour from her hands onto a ruffled apron and smooths a lock of gray hair into the bun at the nape of her neck. She fits the impression I have of the hard-working Mrs. Crowley.

'Mrs. Crowley?' I say. 'Hazel Crowley?'

'No, I'm Mrs. Kingsolver.'

That's not the reply I was expecting.

'Are you Mr. Kingsolver's sister?'

'He doesn't have a sister. I'm his wife, Agnes.'

'Someone told me Mr. Kingsolver is a widower.'

She laughs out loud.

'I can't imagine who would say that. John and I have been married since high school. As you can see, I'm very much alive.'

'I'm Officer Dunning with the Santa Paulina Police Department. Do you have a woman named Hazel Crowley working for you?'

'No, there's just me and my daughter Mabel. What did you say the woman's name is?'

'Hazel Crowley.'

'That does ring a vague bell. She might be the lady who came by several weeks back looking for work as a domestic, but we manage just fine without outside help.'

'Do you have any idea where else she might have looked for work in this area?'

'No, not the slightest. There isn't that much out this way. The last I saw her, she was walking back toward the crossroads, but that was a few weeks ago, right after Halloween. I remember because I still had jack-o-lanterns sitting on the porch rail.'

'Thank you for your time, Mrs. Kingsolver.'

'Wait here a moment,' she says.

She walks away from the door. When she returns she hands me a big bag of apples.

'Kingsolver pippins,' she says. 'Best in the county.'

I drive back to the highway and park on the shoulder of the road to get my thoughts in order. I shift positions on the car seat, but I've already used up all of the comfortable ones.

Hazel Crowley has been lying, or Walter has been lying, or they've both been lying. But why? What I don't need is another missing person on my hands.

Walter says Hazel walks to work, that Kingsolver picks her up or she hitches a ride. The only thing between the King-solver's and the crossroads, other than agricultural land, is Sparkey's Roadhouse. What the hell. I haven't eaten since breakfast and I can sure go for a beer.

It's dark as I pull into the lot at Sparkey's, a square purple stucco box with pink and gold neon looped below the eaves and a few quake fractures running up the façade. Lights are on in three shabby trailers that sit on cinder blocks in the mud hole out back. The enticing aroma of grilling meat pulls me through the front door. I walk through thick veils of cigarette smoke to where a big broad-shouldered man is flipping burgers on a flaming grill behind the bar.

The menu on the chalkboard is short. I'm too tired to make big decisions anyway. Burgers. Fries. Beer. When the food arrives I go into attack mode. When I'm through I sit back and relax with beer number two and study my surroundings.

The raspy voice on the jukebox tells a tale of honky-tonk nights, faithless women, and busted hearts. Ain't it the truth. A crowd gathers around the cigarette machine, everybody talking and laughing like they grew up together. I'm wearing my woolen Irish cap like every Tom, Dick and Harry in the bars back in Southie, but the locals wear baseball caps with logos . . . John Deere . . . Hanson's Feed and Seed . . . Ed's Auto Repair.

A woman comes through a rear door, walks down the short hall and takes the empty stool next to mine. She says her name is Lucille and I buy her a beer. She's a bleached blonde in her thirties with more miles on her odometer than a long-haul truck driver.

'Hazel working tonight?' I ask.

'She's out back.'

That was easy. Blondie has my undivided attention.

'She'll be back in about ten minutes.' She pops a husky laugh. 'Scratch that. She's with Reggie Perkins. She'll be back in five.'

Hooker humor. I can't help smiling.

'You new around here?' she asks.

'I am.'

'You talk funny.'

'We all talk funny in Boston.'

'You work out at the quarry?'

The big man in the chef's apron walks over. There's a broad grin on his face as he scoops up my empty burger basket and leaves my money on the bar.

'Lucille,' he says, 'I've come to put you out of your misery before you get in any deeper. This is the new guy just signed on with the department.'

He holds out his hand. 'Sparkey

137

Bohannon.' We shake.

'Jack Dunning,' I say. 'Tunney told me there are no secrets in this town.'

'I saw you get out of Axel Teague's Caddy. You might as well wear a sign.'

'You going to cause trouble?' asks Lucille. 'Sparkey already paid his pound of flesh this month.'

'Not unless you shoot one of your johns,' I say. 'Other than that I try to stay out of other people's business.'

She laughs. A tooth is missing up front. 'In that case you better keep a close eye on me. There's a few deserve shooting.'

A man walks over and taps her on the shoulder.

'You busy, Lucille?'

COOLEY'S SAND AND GRAVEL is embroidered on his cap.

'Never too busy for you, Buzz,' she says, giving me a wink as she climbs down from her stool. 'See you around Jack.'

'Another beer?' says Sparkey.

'Better not.'

'Dinner's on me. Welcome to Santa Paulina.'

'Thanks. I appreciate it. I just want a

word with Hazel, is all.'

Sparkey looks over my shoulder. 'Here she comes now.' He motions her over, tosses my burger basket in the sink and slaps a few more burgers on the grill.

I turn my head as she crosses the room from the hallway. One look at Hazel and I nearly fall off my stool. I didn't know what to expect, but this doesn't come close. Hazel Crowley is tall and gorgeous, something silvery and slinky flowing like water over her slender frame. She has an abundance of natural red hair like her sons, a complexion like cream and eyes so blue you want to drown in them. She slides onto the stool beside me.

'I've been expecting you, Jack,' she says, using my first name like we were lying in bed together.

She picks a Lucky Strike out of a silver cigarette case and puts it between lips the color of wet cherries. Her fingernails are polished the same serious red. I fumble with my Ronson. She steadies my hand and touches the tip of her cigarette to the blue flame. She pulls the smoke deep into her lungs, exhales dragon-like through her nostrils and picks a tiny piece of tobacco from her tongue. I snap my lighter closed and put it back in my pocket. Watching Hazel Crowley smoke a cigarette is better than sex.

'I've been to the Kingsolver's,' I say, as soon as I find my voice. 'You got a big secret, lady. How long you think you can keep this up before your husband finds out?'

She gives me a soft, jaded look.

'He doesn't want to find out. On some level I'm sure he suspects something, but what I do is outside his frame of reference.'

'It's a risky road to go down, Hazel. Risky in more ways than one.'

'I've been down the other roads and they're all dead ends. I do the next thing that needs to be done and this is what needs to be done, Jack. Besides, Walter has always been better with the kids. He doesn't mind cooking and he has the patience of Job.'

'Do you know what's going on with Louise? Do you have any idea where she is?'

'None.' She takes another long pull from her cigarette and lets the smoke drift out between her lips.

'Can I buy you a drink?' I ask.

'I don't drink,' she says. 'I'm a Baptist.' We pass a second or two in silence. 'I expected her to run off with Thad Galadette, like I run off with Walter when I was young and stupid. Since he's still here and she's not, I couldn't venture a guess as to where she is or why.'

'Do you think Thad would hurt her?'

'No. He's head over heels. He's a good kid.'

'What about his father, Grady?'

'I don't like him. I don't trust him. Would he do something to Louise? That's your area of expertise, Jack.'

'I hear he's heavy-handed, likes to have his way.'

She penetrates me with those lethal blue eyes.

'Don't we all, Jack?'

'Was Louise seeing anyone other than Thad?'

'Not that I know of, but I don't know that I can say the same for Thad.'

'What do you mean?' I say, leaning closer, feeling the animal heat rising off her skin.

'Open your eyes, Jack. Somebody's little darling swallowed a pumpkin seed.'

9

Dangerous Revelations

As soon as Escobar walks out the door, Angel and Rosalita go upstairs to Angel's room and look out the window. The men are having a heated exchange by the garage. The tension between them is palpable even from a distance.

'I wish we could hear what they're saying,' says Rosalita. 'I wonder if they're arguing about us.'

They watch Fritz walk down the driveway and swing open the double gate. Escobar revs the engine of his convertible and almost runs Fritz over as he blasts past him on his way down the hill toward town.

'What do you know about Fritz?' asks Angel.

'Not much. He was once Señor Escobar's bouncer at El Toro before he was hired on here as security. He has a lot of bodybuilding trophies in his room. Sometimes we talk when Señor is not around. I think he likes me. Maybe he likes me much.'

It's hard for Angel to imagine more than a few monosyllabic grunts coming from Fritz, but he might come out of his shell because of Rosalita's gentle, disarming manner. Maybe he knows what's going on. Maybe he knows about the baby and where he is.

'Tell me about your baby, Rosalita? How was he taken from you?'

'I am told not to talk about it if I want to get him back.'

'Whatever you tell me won't go beyond this room. If I know what's going on, maybe I can help you. Maybe we can help each other.'

'We were smuggled across the border at San Isidro, my husband Hector, myself and little Matías. There were thirty of us hidden in the back of a furniture van. Everyone paid all the money they had to come to America for a better life. Already I am sorry. At least in Mexico we had family and neighbors.

Now I have no one.'

'Where did you learn to speak English so well?'

'My mother's grandparents were part of the Mormon migration to Mexico after Utah gained statehood, so several of us are passably bilingual.'

'I see. Where is your husband Hector now?'

'We were going from one small café to the next near Pershing Square. Hector hoped to find a job as a dishwasher. It was about ten o'clock at night and we did not yet have a place to stay. A man jumped out of an alley and stabbed my husband. He fell to the sidewalk. Before I could figure out what was happening the man snatched my baby from my arms and ran back the way he came.

'I didn't know what to do. I knelt down beside my Hector. Another stranger appeared out of nowhere. It was Señor Escobar. He chased the man but lost him in the back alleys. By the time he returned, Hector was dead and the police were coming. In Mexico we are afraid of the police. They lock you up for no reason and make your family pay to get you out.

''Quick, come with me,' said the stranger, 'or you will be arrested and sent back to Mexico. Then you will never see your baby again.' I hesitate. I don't want to go with a stranger. I don't want to leave the body of my husband, but I am more afraid of jail and never seeing Matías again. 'I will help you get your baby back,' he says, and so I go with him. It has been two weeks and all I get are promises.'

'So that's how you ended up here.'

'He said that I can stay here in the big house if I am willing to cook and clean until I get my son back. It seems a small price to pay. I have nowhere else to go.'

'Except the price has gone up and your baby's not back,' says Angel.

Rosalita drops her eyes, her hands folded in her lap. She has a calm, dignified beauty. She may have been raised in a poor Mexican village, but she's been properly raised.

'How old is your baby, Rosalita?'

'He is eight months and just beginning

to crawl. He will be so afraid without me, Angel.'

'Would it surprise you to know it was an orange-haired man who stole my purse at the train station and that Mr. Escobar is the one who came to my rescue?'

'I don't understand. How can that be possible?'

'They're behind all this, Mr. Escobar and the orange-haired man. It's a setup to get us to this house.'

'Why? What's in it for them?'

'That's something we need to think about. It could be any number of things, none of them good.'

'Are you going to town today? Are you going to leave me alone?'

'No, I don't trust Fritz to take me where I want to go. Mr. Escobar could be setting me up. Besides, that twenty dollars is all I have and we might need it for something else. Has he given you any money?'

'None.'

'Then we have to be careful with what little we have. Rosalita, I need you to do something. It's a beautiful day. Go sit by the fountain and enjoy the sun.'

'Are you coming with me?'

'No, but I'm not leaving this house until we get your baby back. Go strike up a conversation with Fritz. Ask him if he knows anything about an orange-haired man.'

'I don't know if I can do this.'

'Rosalita, just sit by the fountain and look pretty. Now go.'

Ever since Angel arrived at Eagle Crest, something has been bothering her. After Rosalita leaves she goes to the closet, gathers up the shoes and tosses them on the bed. There are expensive shoes for every occasion . . . glittery high heels . . . Italian leather sandals . . . elegant flats . . . English riding boots and tennis shoes. They range from size five to nine. A lady's dress size may change but not the length of her feet.

She tosses everything back in the closet. There is no Julia, no daughter in college and probably no dead wife. There never has been, or there would be a picture on a wall . . . a framed high school diploma . . . a wedding album . . . something.

Angel is Julia and she is certainly not the first. How many other Julias have slept in this bed and worn these clothes? More importantly, where are they now? Angel could probably make her escape, but she can't leave Rosalita behind, and Rosalita can't go anywhere without first getting her baby back. When Angel was desperate for rescue, Jack came into her life. Maybe she can help Rosalita like Jack helped her.

Angel walks to the window and looks into the courtyard. Fritz is sitting beside Rosalita at the fountain. A leaf spirals down from an oak tree and settles in her hair. Fritz reaches over and gently removes it.

An hour later she returns to the house.

'Angel, the orange-haired man took Fritz's place as bouncer at El Toro when Fritz started asking too many questions about what was going on there. His name is Dutch Hackett. Fritz promises to do a little poking round for us.'

'That's a good place to start, Rosalita.

See how easy that was.'

That evening as she and Rosalita sit down to a dinner of scampi and asparagus shoots, Rick walks in unexpectedly. Rosalita sets a plate in front of him. There is no 'thank you,' no sign of gratitude. His frigid silence ices her out of the room and she exits in a swirl of full skirts and jingling jewelry.

'You have no right to treat her like a piece of furniture,' says Angel.

Escobar looks surprised, then gives a casual shrug.

'She's a servant. Servants do not eat in the main dining room when I am at the table.' He sits quietly for a moment. 'You're right. I've had a hard day. I'll make it up to her.'

By staying out of her bedroom? By returning her child?

He studies Angel from across the table. The bruising on her face is no longer noticeable beneath a sheer patina of powder. The frightened little ragamuffin he picked up at the train station has undergone a transformation. She wears a rose silk dress and a faint whisper of cologne, her table manners polished and precise. In the stillness of the room and the wavering candlelight, he finds her intriguing.

'You're staring,' she says, setting her fork on the edge of her plate with a decisive click.

'You're just so lovely in the candlelight.'

'I'm trying to make up for a less than stellar first impression. It isn't every day a lady is robbed of her money within five minutes of getting off a train.'

Escobar doesn't remember feeling this way about the others who'd come and gone from this house. They lacked dimension compared to the girl who sits across from him. The problem is — and it's a big problem — he's already made a commitment regarding her future. In his world, a deal is a deal. To back out now would be dangerous, if not suicidal.

'Fritz tells me you didn't shop after all.'

'I wasn't in the mood. Maybe tomorrow.'

'I think you're beginning to feel at home here.'

'I haven't decided how I feel yet.'

'Tomorrow evening I see Mr. Horvat. Soon you'll have a job and a place of your own — unless of course, you'd like to stay on here. It's not like I don't have the room, and it would be nice to have someone to talk to.'

'It's peaceful enough. It's something to think about, isn't it?'

There's something captivating about this girl. She's innocently seductive and at the same time resistant enough to get his hormones churning. Besides, he's tiring of the Mexican girl. He likes to keep things fresh and full of discovery.

'Let's say we invite him for dinner and you can discuss the job. Certainly it's worth waiting a day or two. If he likes your qualifications he'll pay you well.'

The last thing he wants is to bring him here, but the promise of a job will buy him more time with Angel, and Horvat will be curious enough to want to play along. If he's lucky Escobar can talk himself out of the whole deal.

'Yes, but only a day or two. Where's his office?'

'What?'

'His accounting office. You said he's an accountant.'

'Down on Sunset somewhere. It's in the nice part of town.'

Did she notice his hesitation?

The more he sees of Angel, the more he wants to keep her here; but between her and Horvat, he's walking a tightrope without a safety net. Bottom line, he doesn't want to give this one up.

He recalls something his father once told him: 'A woman will make you happy if she is proficient in one of two rooms, the kitchen or the bedroom.'

If he can persuade Angel to stay, she'll never have to cook a meal or wash a dish. He'll put her in a bed the size of a swimming pool and never let her up for air. If he can't persuade her to stay, he'll take stronger measures.

Rick checks his watch and sets his napkin on the table.

'I have business in town. Give my apologies to Rosalita. I have no excuse for my rudeness, except I've become uncivil from living alone.

The next day Mr. Escobar works on his ledgers at El Toro, making sure nobody is dipping into the till and that the girls aren't squirreling away money in their girdles and wigs. Then he drives to Venice beach and has dinner in a restaurant where he can watch the waves roll in and think about the best way to handle Horvat.

Rosalita and Fritz spend time talking and walking in the garden. The three of them go over their options and agree that the most important thing is finding Matías Márquez.

★ ★ ★

Bobo Horvat is 500 pounds of pale, sweaty dough, rising in the California heat. When he bathes in his over-sized tub, it takes three of his fancy-boys to haul him out. Despite liberal soapings, he still smells like a wet dog.

This however, does not deter his clientele, since he's the go-to person for illicit merchandise of the human variety. If their pockets are deep enough, he'll fill a special order for a runaway girl or a promising street boy. He uses his power of persuasion ... food ... drugs ... a place to sleep. He's not above snatching kids off the street provided they still have a fresh bloom about them.

Anyone who thinks slavery ended with the Emancipation Proclamation is delusional. If his clients are rich enough and desperate enough, he can sometimes fill an order for a baby. Blue eyes or brown? Dark-skinned or fair? Their wish is his command ... for a price.

Where the hell is Escobar? The night is warm and windy and moonlit. If they can wrap up their business, it's still early enough for a 'flutter' with some wistfully graceful young lad in the leafy Eden of Pershing Square.

It's past midnight. Bobo works on his third tequila at the El Toro bar, his butt swallowing the stool that struggles to support his whaleness. It is not a noisy bar, but a place of uneasy silences, shadows and whispers, where debts are incurred and collected and deals are sealed with a nod, a handshake and a concealed weapon in a waistband or boot.

Ricardo Escobar enters the door of his establishment like a movie star walking the red carpet. He radiates charm and nonchalance, wearing sunglasses after dark, his fingers glittering with diamond rings. Despite his carefree demeanor, Bobo senses that his partner in crime is off his game tonight.

Escobar sits on the stool to Bobo's left. The bartender brings him tequila and walks to the far end of the bar.

'You're late,' says Bobo.

'I've been rethinking our deal.'

'It's too late for that.'

'I spoke prematurely. I'm not sure the girl is right for your client after all.'

'Yesterday she was a virgin princess, remember? Hair like spun moonlight and eyes like violets in the rain. I hope you're not telling me some cataclysmic event has taken place in the last twenty-four hours? She come down with measles or the clap?'

'Don't be crude. It's just that it doesn't

156

feel right anymore.'

'For god sake, don't go sentimental on me. It feels right to Prince Abdul Akbar Aziz, the diplomat who's flying back to Saudi in a few days.'

Escobar cuts him a sharp glance.

'You've got to be kidding. Don't tell me you can't back out of this.'

'Back out of it? Are you nuts? He's already put half the money down on my word alone. This is just the client we've been waiting for. Where he's from, men are allowed four wives and an unlimited number of concubines. Think of the implications for future transactions.'

'I don't like the idea of dealing with foreigners.'

'Think of it this way. Once she's gone, we're safely out of it. No one will find her unless they ride a camel over a hundred miles of sand.' He shakes his head. 'Can you imagine The Allies giving an entire nation to one family? Boggles the mind, don't it?'

'She's an orphan. No one is looking for her.'

Bobo pulls a piece of paper from his

pocket. He unfolds it and spreads it on the bar. It's a missing persons flyer out of Santa Paulina, California. A blow-up of Angel's face is dead center. She's a minor, from Santa Paulina. Sandy blonde hair. Blue eyes. Five foot three. Ninety-nine pounds.

'Sound familiar?' says Bobo.

Escobar breaks into a sweat. Bobo enjoys seeing him squirm, his invulnerability fraying around the edges. He grins. Chalk one up for the fat man.

'I think you can see that getting her out of the country is the best solution,' says Bobo. 'We can't afford to be caught with her.' Escobar drinks down his tequila, his hands cold and a bit unsteady. 'Don't look so glum. There's a dozen more where this one came from.'

'When you see her, you may not think so,' says Escobar, feeling the uncomfortable shift of power in their relationship.

'All that delicious blondeness? The Prince will be delighted. Don't forget, come the weekend, the Garcias are flying in from Tucson for the baby. Make sure Dutch has him ready to go.'

'All right, all right, I just want to get this over. Angel thinks you're coming to offer her a job. I'll expect you for dinner tomorrow around eight. Bring the Prince so there won't be any misunderstandings. Take her when you leave or you don't take her at all. Is that understood?'

'We'll be there. In the mean time adjust your attitude. Business is business. After we close the deal we'll be richer than God.'

'After this deal I'm retiring. I don't have the stomach for it anymore.'

Horvat leaves and Escobar drains a couple more tequilas.

'Another drink, Señor Escobar?' says the bartender.

'No, José. I'm going home.'

He's heading out the door when the phone rings and José calls him back. It's Horvat.

'What now?'

'We'll see you on Friday, instead. I forgot tomorrow is Thanksgiving. I have to be at my grandmother's house.'

'People like you don't have grandmothers,' mutters Escobar, hanging up the phone. He climbs back on the bar stool.

'Oh, what the hell . . . Make it one more for the road.'

★ ★ ★

Fritz waits until Escobar leaves and the lights go out upstairs. He's tired of taking orders. In fact, he's tired of the whole damn setup. He abandons his post and cruises east on Sunset into the downtown. It's a district of old brick business buildings, seedy hotels, sleazy bars and alleys you enter at your own risk even during the day. It's where the strong prey on the weak and 'respectable' people lose their public personas to satisfy their darker fantasies.

After hearing Rosalita's story, he's convinced that Escobar is involved in more than run-of-the-mill lechery and vice. Fritz thought he'd seen it all when he worked security at El Toro . . . bootleg booze . . . gambling . . . loan-sharking . . . extortion . . . slots and prostitution. When he thought there might be something even darker going on, his suspicions got him 'promoted' to security at Eagle Crest.

Fritz turns onto a dark side street off Pershing Square and follows the mariachi music pouring out of a streetside café. He parks where he can watch the front of El Toro. On the broken sidewalk out front, lumpy hookers in oversized earrings and undersized skirts smoke and argue and strut their stuff in torn fishnet stockings and rundown shoes. No haute couture here. Then again, the men they take upstairs are unlikely to be fashion critics. He sees the Italian woman, Alba, loop her arm around a man's waist and escort him inside. Alba kept house at Eagle Crest until Rosalita took her place. This does not bode well for the young Mexican mother's future.

Escobar's M.G. is parked at the curb behind Horvat's flashy yellow Caddy. The fat queen is the first to leave, rolling out the door and driving toward the park with a self-satisfied grin on his face. By the time Dutch Hackett appears, Fritz has smoked his last cigarette. He lets Dutch get two blocks on him before he pulls into traffic. He separates himself from the

Ford coupé by three cars at the risk of losing him; but if they think he's on to them, he'll never get a second chance to find Rosalita's baby.

They drift through South-Central, a rough, mostly black section of town, and turn into a residential neighborhood a few blocks before Slausen. Dutch pulls in front of a pink stucco box as Fritz hangs back at the corner. He knocks on the door and a woman in a shapeless cotton robe lets him in.

It's a street of broken-down clothes-lines, overflowing backyard incinerators, garbage-strewn vacant lots and chain-link fences. Fritz backtracks and drives down the alley behind the house. He squeezes between the neighbor's fence and the pink house and peeks through a side window beneath a torn shade.

Dutch sits in a chair across from an elderly white couple seated on a green overstuffed sofa. They chat congenially. He opens his wallet and hands them a couple bills. The elderly man puffs on a pipe. The woman's knitting is in her lap. Everything seems so damn normal. Then from the hall a middle-aged bottle-blond appears carrying a baby. He's dressed in blue corduroy overalls and a white t-shirt. He's a smiling Mexican baby with big brown eyes and curly dark hair. Matías Márquez.

Just as Fritz is settling into surveillance mode a side door bursts open in the adjacent house, capturing Fritz in a square of light. A seismic little terrier flies out and throws himself against the chain link fence with unearthly shrieks and the gnashing of teeth. A man appears in the doorway. He's a seven-foot-tall black man.

'Peeping Tom!' he hollers and a bullet flies past Fritz's ear, kicking a piece of stucco off the wall and into his eye. He opens the gate and sics the beast on Fritz.

Fritz runs toward his car, dragging the dog on the cuff of his pants. He flings open the car door, popping the terrier in the ribs. The dog flies through the air and rolls over a couple times in the dust. A bullet hits his trunk as he roars down the alley. When he pulls onto the street and looks in the rear view, the dog is chasing his car.

The wind is up, the leaves cartwheeling through the moonlit night, when Escobar passes through the unlocked gate and snugs the M.G. between the Bentley and Fritz's Chevy. When he opens the car door, he notices the hot engine smell in the air. He touches the hood of the Chevy. It's warm. His anxiety level ratchets up a notch. He knocks on Fritz's door. Fritz answers in his pajamas.

'What is it, Boss?'

'You left your post tonight.'

'I needed motor oil. The stores are closed tomorrow.'

'What about the girls?'

'I waited until they were asleep.'

'Don't leave your post again without express permission.'

Fritz goes back inside and the deadbolt scrapes into place.

Escobar takes the gate key from the nail on the back wall. He walks to the gate and padlocks the chains in place, then drops the key in his pocket.

* * *

It isn't until the next day, when Escobar drives to town to pick up a ready-made turkey dinner from the Beverly Hills Hotel, that Fritz and Rosalita steal a private moment by the fountain. She wears a long pink dress, her slender waist cinched with a silver concha belt, her long black hair shining in the sun.

'Rosie, I found your baby.'

'Oh God,' she says, trembling, holding back tears. 'Is he all right?'

'Yes, he's fine. He's a beautiful little boy, Rosalita. He's with a family in South-Central. Dutch was there. Through the window I saw him hand the people money. I don't think they have any idea how they're being used. The next-door neighbor caught me peeping and took a potshot at me so I had to make a run for it.'

'How are we going to get Matías back? Should we call the police?'

'If we do we'll get bogged down in endless red tape. They'll hold him in protective custody until they check your immigration status and see his birth certificate and . . . '

'Fritz, he has no certificate. He was born at home, fifty miles from the nearest hospital.'

'I'm getting you out of here tomorrow when Escobar is distracted. We'll get the baby and I'll drive you home.'

'All the way to Mexico?'

'All the way.'

'You would do that for me?'

'Rosalita, I'll do anything you ask me to.' That brings a blush to her face and what passes for a smile to Fritz's stolid Germanic features.

'What about Angel? We can't leave her here.'

'Be sensible. The baby first. Then we'll worry about Angel.'

10

Letting Go of the Past

I leave Sparkey's with a sense of foreboding. I drive back over the bridge into Santa Paulina and pull up in front of the Do Drop Inn on Lower Shannon Street. It's a dreary hole-in-the-wall squeezed between a plumbing supply outfit and an auto wrecking yard.

I try to control my limp as I walk through the door. The joint is a serious watering hole, no food available unless you count the bowl of dill pickles and a jar of hardboiled eggs sitting at one corner of the bar. There's a shuffleboard game, two pinball machines, a jukebox, and the rattle and thump of leather dice cups slamming against the bar as customers roll for drinks. There's probably a card game in progress in the back room and a couple of slots, but I'm not a vice cop and have no desire to be one.

'So what'll it be?' says the bartender. He's a tough old bird with a yellow pallor and arms covered with liver spots.

'I'm Jack Dunning. I'm looking for a couple by the name of Kapp.'

'You a cop?'

'I'm a consultant with the department.'

He pretends to think hard and shakes his head.

'They're from the encampment by the river,' I tell him.

'What you want to talk to them about?'

'Mind if we stop dancing around? It's a domestic issue.'

'You probably mean Fergus and Viola, but they're not around anymore.'

'What do you mean by that — not around?'

'They shoved off yesterday. Hitched a ride with a guy on his way to Castroville to harvest Brussels sprouts.'

'Where's Castroville?'

'On the coast, about sixty miles south of San Francisco.'

'That's over a hundred miles from here.'

'So it is.'

'They say anything about coming back this way?'

'With those two, I wouldn't count on it.'

'Their tent is still pitched by the river. Their child is living in it.'

'That must be why they left it behind.'

'Must be. Thanks for your cooperation . . . '

'Angus. Angus Coopersmith. Just call me Gus.'

I consider circling back to the encampment to talk with Eleanor, but it's cold and late and everyone will be settled in for the night. No sense getting the dogs barking and everybody riled up when I can deal with it in the morning.

I park in the alley behind The Rexford and go through the rear entrance to the lobby. Hank is drinking coffee and going over the ledgers. A few men sit in the lobby smoking and playing checkers. Hank looks at me over the top of his glasses.

'Jack, I thought you skipped town. How's the case going?'

'I'm still trying to get a handle on it. I hope I'm not screwing things up for you.

I was supposed to be working cold cases and all of a sudden I'm in the middle of a hot potato.'

'No, everything's been dead around here, just the way I like it.' He closes the ledger and sets it aside. 'You've got a visitor in your room. I hope you don't mind my letting her in.'

'Angel?' I say, my heart rolling over in my chest.

'Sorry Jack. It's the other one.'

'Sandra?'

'That's the only other one I know of.'

'I don't think I'm ready for this. Wonder what she wants.'

'Probably money. Isn't that what they all want?'

'Then she'd call. Why come all the way from Boston?'

'You're asking a guy with three ex-wives? I never could figure out the female mind. How could I? I spent all my time down at the gym bringing along the next golden boy. Who knows, maybe you'll get lucky. What if she won the Irish Sweepstakes and she's come to split the winnings?'

'Lucky? That's the one part of being Irish that hasn't panned out.'

We share a cynical laugh and I head up the elevator. I stand outside the door of my room, take a deep breath and roll tension from my shoulders.

'Come in, Jack. I know you're there.' That's the kind of woman Sandra is — viscerally intuitive, especially when it comes to the places I hide bottles and the brand of whiskey on my breath. I open the door and walk in.

Sandra looks like a million bucks in a rust wool sheath with matching coat. She wears shiny black high heels, black kid gloves and a necklace of elephant pearls. Her champagne-blonde hair is upswept from her slender neck with every strand in place. I wanted her to look a bit unraveled, like regret at having dumped me kept her awake nights. Alas, she looks better than she did the last five years of our marriage.

'I'm surprised to see you here, Sandra.'

'Herbert has an elderly aunt in Stockton who's in failing health and he'd like to see her one more time, so we might as well kill two birds with one stone.' She draws two sets of documents from her leather bag and sets them on top of the bureau.

'Sign beside the red 'x',' she says.

I pick up the pen she hands me and I sign. 'What are these?'

'It's my Declaration of Independence.' She gives me a tight-lipped look. 'They're the final divorce papers, what do you think they are?' She tears off my copy and returns the duplicates to her bag.

'I thought it would take longer than this,' I say. 'We haven't dealt with the issue of alimony yet.'

'That won't be necessary. Herbert and I are getting married in Nevada on our return trip.'

I should be relieved at having dodged the 'A' bullet. Instead I'm depressed that someone else is doing well at something I failed so miserably at.

She addresses the second set of documents. 'Sign by the black arrow,' she says. I sign. She tears off my copy and hands it to me. 'These are the closing papers on the Sandford Street house. I'll mail them from the post office in the morning. As soon as they arrive at the real estate office, they'll cut you a check and send it here to The Rexford.' She folds the remaining papers and puts them in her bag with the others.

'What about your half?' I ask.

'I want no association with that dump, financially or otherwise. We'll be residing in Herbert's haute moderne by the lake.'

'My house is not a dump, Sandra. It's a . . .'

I already sound like a defensive fool and stop talking.

'That concludes our dealings unless I've overlooked something,' she says. She looks at me with lucid gray eyes set in the first face I ever loved. Over the years I changed a soft, loving girl into the angry, wounded woman who stands before me. An arrow twists in my heart.

I reach out and touch her gloved hand.

'I wish you and Herbert the best,' I say. 'I'm sorry if I ever . . .'

'You're pathetic, Jack,' she says, jerks her hand away and walks past me out the door.

Sandra leaves the door open and I close it. I stand by the window and watch Herbert open the passenger side door to his new Lincoln. When she appears he kisses her lightly on the cheek, makes sure her coat doesn't get caught in the door, then closes it. It's the last time I will see or hear from her.

* * *

Cookie can't sleep. The wind is up and she paces the comfortable parlor in her chenille robe and fluffy slippers, getting more irritated and angry by the moment. Where is the call from Chief Garvey in response to her note? Why hasn't she heard from the new officer who's handling the Louise Crowley case? She knows they're working the auction barn homicide, but no matter how much time passes the victim will never be less dead and the lady lying in the woods might still be alive.

Tonight Cookie feels very alone. Joe locked up and went home an hour ago so he could prepare for tomorrow's feast.

He'll pick her up in the morning and they'll spend the day out at his place. Cookie goes to the phone and calls the police station. After ten rings a heavily accented male voice answers.

'To whom am I speaking?' she says, in her school teacher voice.

'Manuel Cardones, Señora, the night janitor.'

'The night janitor? Where is everybody?'

'They booked someone for the auction barn murder, so they've all gone home.'

'Judas Priest!' she says. 'What about the Crowley girl?'

'Who?'

That's all it takes. The zigzag pattern begins to flicker behind her right eye and she knows the migraine has begun. She hangs up the phone. Even with her eyes closed she sees a flashing mandala of light. She fires off a few well-chosen expletives that her father resorted to when his tractor broke down or his milk cow went dry.

* * *

Manuel goes about his business. He'd like to help the lady, but he's a janitor, not a policeman. He takes his long-handled feather duster and whisks the cobwebs from the ceiling fixture. A crumpled piece of paper tumbles downward from above the front desk. He smooths it out on the desktop and squints at it, but since he can't read, it's impossible to determine its importance. If it was important, why would it be dangling from the edge of the light cover? He considers taking it out with the trash. Then again, if he is wrong he could lose the job he needs to support his family. He decides to play it safe.

Manuel studies the name plates on the desks in the squad room, but can't read them either. He puts the note on top of the desk with the least cluttered top. That way it's bound to get noticed.

*   *   *

Minutes after the flashing lights begin, the pain hits with staggering intensity. Normally Cookie would scurry for her bottle of magic elixir at the first sign of

176

trouble. This time she resists her first impulse. The last time she took the drug her psychic vision had been incomplete, like a radio message garbled by static. Who is the assailant? Where in the vast expanse of woods had the lady been attacked? Maybe the drug was creating interference. Tonight Cookie decides a different approach might result in a better outcome.

She walks across the room to the round table that holds her crystal ball. She fights a dizzying swirl of nausea as she lowers herself slowly onto the velvet-cushioned chair. She contemplates the orb as it gazes back at her from its resting place of midnight blue. Of course, it has no real power . . . but then again . . . the more she looks the more it has . . . well . . . something.

She reaches out and draws the ball closer. At first she moves her fingers over the cool, smooth surface. Sprays of bubbles are trapped in the glass like a universe of miniature stars. With a sigh she places her palms on the ball and surrenders to its mystery. She has nothing to lose and if she makes a fool of herself, so what? There's no one around to see.

Cookie's eye reddens and swells shut, but the less she sees of the room around her the more she sees an aerial panorama of Santa Paulina and its surrounding countryside. She closes her good eye and soars upward on a current of air. An eagle's view of river and woodland opens beneath her. An overgrown logging road and an abandoned mansion left to crumble in the elements, come into view. Through a canopy of winter-stripped trees, she sees what she's looking for . . . or thinks she does . . . not with her mortal eyes, but through the fingertips that transmit energy from the crystal ball to her inner eye. It's as if a road map has been spread in front of her. She knows where to go and what to do.

★   ★   ★

I was exhausted when I arrived home. I was looking forward to a hot shower and a good night's sleep, not a face-to-face with an ex-wife who was supposed to be several thousand miles away. I stood there in my dirty second-hand cowboy boots while she looked like a model in the pages of a fashion magazine.

I lie awake late into the night thinking about Sandra's visit, listening to the wind whistle through the eaves and the plumbing clank deep in the skeleton of the building, regretting all the good things I've let slip through my fingers. It's an easy pit to fall into between midnight and dawn. Looking back, I've only been good at one thing in my life. I'm a damn good cop. With Angel gone and Louise Crowley still missing, I won't allow that part of me to be eroded by self-doubt.

At 4:00 a.m., two Mexican chaps down the hall turn on mariachi music as they get ready for the early shift at the cannery. I drag myself out of bed and knock on their door. When they open it, I raise an eyebrow and say nothing. I must have broken the language barrier because the one called Felipe says, '*Si*, Meester Doonig,' and snaps off the radio. I nod and go back to smoking and staring at the ceiling. I doze off sometime before dawn.

Albie brings the morning paper and I give him a tip for getting my tired butt out of the sack. I bundle up and pull on my cowboy boots. Today I snap Teague's pistol into my shoulder holster and strap it over my cable-knit sweater. I can't say why I'm doing this, except for the uneasy stirring I feel in my gut when something's about to break in a case. I climb into my sheepskin jacket and bump into Jake outside my door.

'I hope you can make it by the church later. We start serving dinner at three,' he says.

'What's the occasion?' I ask.

'Where you been man? It's Thanksgiving.' He walks away laughing and shaking his head.

Jim Tunney is gabbing with Hank when I take the elevator to the lobby.

'Something going on I should know about?' I ask.

'We solved the auction barn homicide last night.'

'That's great,' I say, filling my thermos from the coffee urn at the end of the counter. 'Who done it?'

'The victim's best friend. They got stupid drunk the night of the cock fight. Now, he can't remember if they were fighting over a woman or a rooster.'

'That's pathetic,' says Hank, 'although I get the rooster part.' We start the day with a laugh.

'Anyway,' says Jim, 'I'm at loose ends. I've got no wife to cook me a turkey and I don't want to spend the day sitting around the squad room with Swack and Green.'

'Come out to the encampment with me. I can use a second perspective on the Louise Crowley case. There's also the issue of an abandoned teenager to deal with.'

'Okay, I'll follow you out.'

* * *

Walter Crowley rises early to start the fire in the stove. He looks over at his little red-haired boys who are curled into one another on the mattress like a litter of prize-winning pups. He's neither a permissive nor demonstrative man, but he loves his children beyond the limits of endurance, including the one who's missing.

At this hour, Louise would be getting the boys up and helping the younger ones dress as he made breakfast. Danny would be coming out from behind the stove, yawning and stretching. The dog's absence is not only confusing, but leaves one more crack in the family circle. And what about Hazel? She didn't make it home again last night. He prepares himself for the day she won't come back at all. It will probably be sooner than later.

He touches a match to the pyramid of crumpled paper and kindling on the grate and goes to the back of the room for a few more scraps of wood. As he reaches for a piece of two-by-four, he stops and looks around. Something is missing. It's the heirloom egg basket that was woven by his great-grandmother.

Walter gently shakes his oldest boy from sleep.

'What is it paw-paw?'

'Teddy, have you seen great-grandma's basket?'

*   *   *

Joe arrives to pick up Cookie on Thanksgiving morning and finds her still in bed. She sighs and rolls over. There's swelling around her eye and he knows she's had another bad night.

'Not again, Cookie. You should have called me.'

'Make a pot of coffee, would you dear, while I pull myself together. I need a ride to the police station. I know where to find Louise Crowley, but we can't waste any time.'

'Another vision?' he asks.

'Yes Joe, and this time I know exactly where to look.'

Cookie is unsteady, but within an hour she stands in front of Officer Swackhammer with Joe Crisalli at her side. She wears her red wool coat and hat and a warm muffler around her neck.

'What is it this time?' says Swack. 'The Chief won't be pleased if you're beating the same old drum.'

Swack is in a bad mood this morning. He and Green are on the roster when the rest of the world is home eating turkey and stuffing.

'Listen,' says Joe, 'is it asking too much to expect a response to Cathleen's note? We do, after all, pay your salaries.'

'Give me a piece of paper,' says Cookie. She has a fierce look in her eye that Swack decides not to challenge. He hands her a pencil and a piece of typing paper as Green watches from an adjacent desk. Cookie sketches a hasty map of an old logging road a mile or so west of the encampment. A scribbled star a few hundred feet from the road marks the location of the missing Louise Crowley.

'If the Chief wants to find that girl, this is where she is and this is where we'll be,' she says.

'Come on Cookie, let's get out of this insane asylum,' says Joe.

As soon as they're gone, Swack folds the map into a paper airplane and sails it across the room.

'You're a sick son of a bitch,' says Green.

* * *

I pull to a stop in front of the encampment and Jim parks behind me in the black-and-white. On the drive over I filled him in on what I'd done on the case to date. A couple dogs amble over, sniff a greeting and walk away. Neither one is Danny. At the far end of the camp I see Grady and Thad Galadette working under the hood of the flatbed. Walter Crowley is standing by his door. Jim and I walk over.

'Mr. Crowley, this is Officer Tunney. He's here to offer his expertise on your daughter's case.'

'Well, come on in. Two heads are better than one. I have something to tell you fellows.'

We follow him inside. The youngsters are sitting on the mattress eating oatmeal with butter and brown sugar. Walter wastes no time telling us about the missing basket and how Louise must have

185

taken it with her the day she vanished.

'My boy Teddy said Louise was going to surprise me one of these days by bringing me mushrooms for my stew. I can't think of anything other than food that would compel her to go to the woods in the rain.

'Now Louise wouldn't know an edible mushroom from a death cap but Eleanor would. I tried to wake her up this morning but she won't answer. I went to the woods alone but I'd have to know where to look. Maybe she'd get up if you tried.'

'We need to talk to her anyway. I think her parents may have skipped town.'

'Well that's a damn shame. The girl deserves better than what she got.'

★ ★ ★

'This is it,' I tell Jim as we approach the flap of the Kapp tent.

'Eleanor, it's Jack Dunning.'

No response.

'Eleanor Kapp, I need to have a word with you. Please, get up.'

186

I look at Jim and shrug.

'Try the flap,' he says, in a hard whisper.

I do. It's not secured.

'Eleanor, I have Officer Tunney with me. We're coming in.'

I pull back the flap and look inside, giving my eyes a minute to adjust to the darkness. A pile of raggedy blankets on the floor serves as a bed. I step inside. There's no stove and the air is icy.

'Eleanor,' I say once more, this time irritation reflected in my tone. I toss back the blankets. She's not there.

We stand outside the tent trying to decide what to do next.

'Maybe she's gone for water,' I say. 'Come on, I'll introduce you to a couple players in this drama and then we'll go look for her.'

Thad looks up as we approach the truck. Grady stays hidden under the hood.

'Hello, Officer Dunning.'

'Hi, Thad. This if Officer Tunney.' They acknowledge one another with a nod and a handshake.

'We found a battery at the junkyard. We're waiting to see if it holds a charge.'

'That's good Thad. You see Eleanor this morning?'

'Hardly anybody gets up before noon around here. Isn't a lot to get up for.'

I bend down by the front of the truck.

'Mr. Galadette, I need a word with you, sir. It won't take but a . . .'

A high-pitched screech goes up from the direction of the river. It sounds at first like children playing, but as it grows closer, an old woman appears, yelling and waving her arms. She wears a threadbare cardigan, a flowered scarf and sagging bobby socks with worn-out saddle shoes.

Jim and I rush over. She's winded, leaning forward with her hands on her knees, trying to catch her breath.

'Take your time,' says Jim, steadying her with a supportive hand on her arm.

'There's a bundle of clothes by the river bank,' she pants. 'I thought maybe I found myself a nice warm pea coat, 'cept there's a dead girl inside it.'

I look at Jim. 'Eleanor,' I say.

188

Grady doesn't look up from under the hood of his truck, but Thad comes over and puts an arm around the woman's shoulder. 'Come and sit with my mom, Mrs. Spruce. I'll make you a cup of tea,' he says.

Jim and I head down the slope to the river.

11

Following the Vision

Joe pulls to the side of the road next to a weedy trail that winds into the woods. He opens his map and spreads it on the dash. 'This has got to be the old logging road,' he says. 'Doesn't look like anyone's been over it in twenty years.'

'That's the last time this area was logged,' says Cookie.

'I'm not sure how far in we can get with the car.'

'Let's go as far as we can and see what happens. I wish I could be sure this is the right road.'

'It's your vision, Cookie.'

'I know, but it looked different from the air.'

He isn't sure what she means, but he lets it pass.

'Are you sure you're up to this, old gal? I can bring you home and come back.'

'There just isn't time, Joe.'

Joe maneuvers the car over the ruts, the undergrowth crunching and crackling beneath the tires, the car rocking from side to side as it bounces over the rugged terrain. A half-mile in, a fallen pine blocks the road.

'This is all she wrote,' says Joe. 'It's Shank's mare from here.' They get out, walk to the back of the car and retrieve a blanket and thermos of hot chocolate from the trunk. They walk around the fallen tree and into the woods.

★ ★ ★

The encampment is crawling with cops. The mortician, Melvin Platt, who acts as coroner, is bent over the body of Eleanor Kapp.

'Dead as a doornail,' says Platt quietly.

'I noticed that,' says Jim.

'No doubt about it. Cold as yesterday's mashed potatoes.'

'You mind if we dispense with the similes and metaphors?' I say. I glance at Jim, like, who is this nut?

'Anyone know this girl?' says Platt.

'Her name is Eleanor Kapp. K-A-P-P,' I say.

'Age?'

'Seventeen.'

'Her parents around?'

'I'm told they've gone picking somewhere on the coast.'

'Well, that's not good,' says Platt.

'What about cause of death?' asks Chief Garvey.

'The capillaries are broken in her eyes and there's extensive bruising on her throat. I'd say someone wrung her neck like a chicken that stopped laying eggs. You can see where thumbs pressed down and crushed the larynx. A postmortem would reveal a broken hyoid bone, but there's no sense taking it that far. Cause of death: strangulation. Manner of death: homicide. It ain't one of your complicated cases, gentlemen.'

'How long has she been dead?' asks the Chief.

'Now that's where things get a bit tricky. The cold delays the onset of rigor mortis so I can't be precise, but I'd say sometime during the night.'

Platt groans as he rises from his crouched position. 'Somebody load her into the van. I got a bad back.' A couple of strapping onlookers lift the body onto a stretcher and carry it to the road where the van is waiting.

'I'd like to have a minute of your time back at the vehicle,' I say.

'There something you can't ask me here?'

'There is. It's something I don't want broadcast.'

The body is loaded into the van and the three of us walk over together.

'Mr. Platt, I'm in the middle of another investigation that may involve the deceased. I need to know if Eleanor Kapp is pregnant. It could determine the direction my investigation takes.'

He sighs. 'Give me a few minutes with the body. If gestation is less advanced than, let's say three months, we'll have to do an autopsy to be certain.'

'Let's hope that isn't necessary.'

He goes through the door at the back of the van and emerges after about ten minutes.

'It's your lucky day, Officer. I'd say she's about fourteen weeks along. I take it she's a single girl.'

'Yes, she's single.'

The Chief walks up and I fill him in.

'I'll work the homicide,' he says. 'You continue with the missing persons case. That sit with you okay?'

'Yessir. I think we'll discover these two cases are connected.'

'You know if there's any bad blood between the victim and somebody who'd like to see her dead?' asks the Chief.

'Maybe whoever got her pregnant. Some men might find that an inconvenience. She had a grudge against the world, so she wasn't well-liked, except by the missing girl, Louise Crowley. She had words with Grady Galadette yesterday. I don't know what it was about, but he didn't like her hanging around his son. Grady's the one who was working on the flatbed, but I don't see him now.'

'Well, I'll have a talk with him.'

'I'd like to take the son Thad down to the station for questioning,' I say.

'Sure, why not. I'll stick around and

interview some of these folks, see if I can find Mr. Galadette. My wife is going to go through the roof if I'm not back by the time that turkey comes out of the oven. We got relations in from out of town.'

'Speaking of turkey,' says Jim, 'here comes the church bus with food for the encampment. They're already lining up.'

'Just so they don't go trampling over my homicide scene,' says the Chief.

'I'd like to take Jim Tunney with me, sir.'

'You two lads go ahead,' he says, reaching in his pocket and taking a long pull from his flask.

* * *

Except for Don Swackhammer and Bruce Green, the squad room is empty. Thad sits across from me at my desk. Jim leans on the wall behind me, his arms crossed over his chest. Thad gives me a questioning look. He removes his hat and a lock of blond hair tumbles over his forehead.

'I don't know why I'm here,' he says.

'You don't think I killed Eleanor, do you?'

'We need to talk in a quiet place away from the uproar,' I say.

'Talk about what?'

'Can you think of anyone who dislikes Eleanor enough to want her dead?'

'No. She was a pain, but so are a lot of people. You don't go around killing people because they're aggravating.'

'You said you took her to the movies once.'

'Back in April. That was a long time ago.'

'And that was the extent of your involvement with her?'

'Yes. I felt sorry for her because she didn't have any friends. Get to know her and you can see why.'

'Might she have read more into the movie date than you intended?'

'It wasn't a date. We watched a double feature. And yes, she had a crush on me, but as far as I know she got over it.'

'Your dad didn't like her hanging around.'

'You met my dad. You know what he's like.'

'Eleanor was pregnant,' I say, snapping

it on him to see his reaction.

His mouth drops open but nothing comes out. Swackhammer and Green stop typing and fiddling with papers. Finally, he says, 'Are you sure?'

'The coroner is sure.'

'Jeez, I never suspected. I can't imagine anyone thinking about her that way. I mean, the girl's a briar patch. She's really unlikeable.'

'So you're telling me it wasn't you.'

'That's what I'm telling you. Louise is my girl.' He's convincing. I tend to believe him.

'Do you have any idea who might have been involved with her?'

'She doesn't talk to that many people, unless she met someone along the road when she was picking bottles. There's my family talks to her ... the Crowleys ... that's about all I can think of offhand.'

'Let's talk about the day you went into the woods. What do you make of someone taking a pot shot at you?'

'The land is posted. Someone may have taken me for a poacher.'

'What if someone didn't want you finding Louise?'

'Who wouldn't want me finding Louise? It's not logical.'

'Her dad thinks she may have gone looking for mushrooms that day.'

'That makes as much sense as anything, except Eleanor is the one knows where to find them . . . so maybe it doesn't make sense after all.'

I tuck a thought in the corner of my brain reserved for sinister speculations. As I let the thought marinate I find myself fiddling with a piece of paper on my desktop. I turn it over and start to read.

'What the hell! Jim, have a look at this.'

He takes the paper from my hand.

'This was written bloody days ago!' says Jim. 'Swack, you've been on the desk. Has the Chief seen this?'

'It was brought in by that wacky old woman who tells fortunes. He was so busy on the auction barn murder that I didn't think he'd want to be bothered.'

'Since when is that your call to make?'

'All right, don't jump down my throat for crissake.'

Green pushes back from his desk and opens his top desk drawer.

'I have something here I think you should see, Jim.' He pulls out a piece of paper. The creases suggest it had once been folded into a paper airplane.

'You sit back down and stay out of this!' says Swack, his face flushed with heat.

'Not anymore,' says Green. He hands the paper to Jim.

Swack tries to intervene, but I straight-arm him and he backs off.

'I'd settle down if I were you,' I say.

Jim and I study the hand-drawn map.

'Mrs. Cook came in again this morning with Joe from the bakery,' says Green. 'It's true she reads fortunes but a lot of folks think there's something to it. She knew the girl was missing before anybody else did. She said the Crowley girl was knifed in the woods and may still be alive.'

'Where can we find Mrs. Cook?'

'You see that star on the map? That's

where she says Louise Crowley is. That's where she and Joe are now.'

I turn to Jim. 'I gotta get out there,' I say.

'I'm coming too,' says Thad, jumping up and putting on his hat.

'I'd better report back to the Chief,' says Jim, 'so we're all on the same page. I'll meet you out there with a search party.' He swings around and jabs Swack in the chest with his finger. 'You haven't heard the end of this.'

★ ★ ★

'The woods didn't look this big from the air,' says Cookie. 'It seems like we've been walking for hours. I'm glad I wore my practical shoes.'

Joe doesn't always know what Cookie is talking about, but he's very good at 'going along.' 'I should have left you in the car. It's got to be ten degrees colder back here. You lean on my arm if you get tired.'

Wind sweeps the treetops and the dead leaves make a scraping sound. A few hundred yards further up the road an abandoned house comes into view. They stop in front of a hand-painted sign peppered with rusty shotgun dings.

NO TRESPASSING
SURVIVORS WILL BE PROSECUTED

'That's bunk. I saw a picture of that house in the Historical Museum,' says Cookie, looking at the collapsed veranda and crumbling turrets. 'No one has lived out here since Al Lavendera hanged himself from the cupola.'

'No kidding? I hadn't heard that story.'

'Oh yes, he was a rich lumber baron, but he checked out when his wife died in childbirth. I suppose it was a good thing in the long run. The forest has had a chance to grow back.' Cookie looks around. 'I think this is where we go off the road.'

'That's an awfully steep slope,' says Joe. 'You'd better take my hand.' They pick their way downward over the slippery earth and rotting leaves. Joe is careful not to drag the blanket in the dirt. Cookie drops the thermos twice and he retrieves it.

'I'm sorry I'm such a klutz,' she says,

her red hat tilted comically to one side.

'You're doing fine.'

The ground levels out at the bottom of the bank. The temperature drops several more degrees where patches of ice have formed in the shade.

'I think something moved back there in the trees, something big,' says Cookie. 'You don't think there are bears out here, do you?'

'Not that I'm aware of. You shouldn't have told the story about the old house. You creeped yourself out.' Joe looks at his watch. 'If we don't start back in an hour or so, it'll be dark by the time we reach the car.'

'Don't worry. We're almost there . . . I think.'

'Louise!' she calls. 'Louise Crowley!'

'Louise, where are you?' booms Joe.

★   ★   ★

Jim flies down the highway in his black-and-white. On River Road he pulls to the side of the one-lane to let the church van leave. When he arrives at the encampment he sees people going in and out of their shanties with sandwiches. Four little redheaded boys sit on a log eating pumpkin pie. He jumps out of the car and races over to where the Chief is standing beside the flatbed talking to a lady in a wheelchair.

'I told him to wait here a minute, that I have a few questions for him,' says the Chief. 'I turn my back and he pulls a vanishing act.'

'He certainly hasn't vanished, Chief. He's gone into the woods to bag a few squirrels is all,' says Mrs. Galadette.

Jim notices braces on her legs, like she had polio when she was a kid. She pulls a blue shawl tightly around her shoulders, her thinness giving the impression of someone who is perpetually cold.

'You're telling me he has a gun with him?'

'You have to shoot them before you can bag them, Chief,' she says in a lilting southern drawl.

Jim taps him on the shoulder and he turns around.

'What now, Tunney? Can't you see I'm

up to my eyeballs in this mess?'

'We just got information that Louise Crowley is lying off an old logging road back in the woods. Jack and Thad Galadette are on their way out there now. There's also an old couple left to look for her a couple hours back.'

'Old couple? What old couple?'

'Madame Zarina and Joe the baker.'

'For heaven's sake! Well, get some men together and get out there. I got my hands full here.' The Chief turns back to Mrs. Galadette. 'When that husband of yours gets back you better damn well tell him to sit tight. I'm trying to run a homicide investigation here.'

★ ★ ★

I pull down the logging road and park behind a big Buick. Thad and I get out and slam the car doors. I feel the weight of the gun in my holster. I don't know if we're going to find a live girl, a dead girl, or no girl at all. It's the first time I've followed a lead provided by a fortune-teller.

Thad walks over and looks at the downed tree blocking the road. 'If it was you and me we could have moved this out of the way and kept the road clear,' he says. He looks into the Buick. 'They didn't think to leave the keys.'

'We'll have to make the best of it.'

Thad hops effortlessly over the tree and jogs on ahead while I walk around it. I'm close behind him for a quarter-mile before my leg acts up. Thad keeps looking over his shoulder, trying to decide if he should go all out or wait for the crippled guy.

'Go Thad, just go. I'll catch up.'

He runs ahead, leaving me in the dust . . . or the mud, if you will.

By the time I reach the abandoned house, Thad is nowhere in sight. I check the map, find the spot where I detour from the road and follow the footprints of the others, slipping and sliding down the slope. I hear a commotion up ahead and power-limp to the edge of a clearing.

Lying motionless on the ground is Louise Crowley, her dark brown hair fanned around her head. Danny's big furry bulk is stretched protectively across her body. A basket lies nearby and mushrooms are scattered over the ground. Cookie and Joe kneel beside her as Thad coaxes the dog to the ground. Danny lies down at her side and rests his muzzle on her arm.

I drop to one knee and find a pulse in her throat.

'She's alive,' I say. 'I've known people to survive with much weaker pulses than this.'

'My God,' says Thad, 'her coat if covered in blood. She's been stabbed.'

Cookie and Joe cover her with a blanket and begin rubbing circulation into her limbs. Her eyelids flutter and open. They're the same green-gold eyes Cookie remembers from her vision.

'Thad,' she says, 'I knew you'd find me.' Her voice is weak, her skin dehydrated and pale.

'I'm right here. We're going to get you to the hospital.'

'I can't move. Something's broken in my back.' Danny whines and licks her cheek. 'My tongue is so dry I can't swallow. If it weren't for Danny keeping me warm last night I'd be dead.'

Joe helps Louise lift her head and Cookie presses a cup of hot chocolate to her lips. Louise drinks it all. Soon the thermos is empty.

'Who did this to you?' I ask. Tears well in her eyes.

'Eleanor, my best friend.'

'What happened?'

'She thought if I was out of the way, she'd have a chance with Thad. She was desperate to find someone to marry her before her secret came out.'

'She was pregnant.'

'Yes, but the man responsible was already married and that was a big problem.'

'Grady Galadette,' I said.

'Yes. I'm sorry Thad,' says Louise. 'It was your father. I thought I could keep it from you.'

'It's all right, Louise. I'm not surprised at anything he does anymore. At times it's hard to believe he's really my dad.'

Grady Galadette steps into the clearing with a deer rifle. Cookie gasps.

'And I can't believe I sired a kid who carves precious little angels out of wood.'

Thad's head jerks toward his dad. 'It didn't keep you from eating the food those carvings put on the table. If you've come here to finish off the last person who knows your secret you're too late, unless of course you plan on killing all five of us.'

'I should have finished you off the day I took that shot to scare you out of the woods.'

'But you did a good job finishing off Eleanor, didn't you?' I say, drawing his attention away from the others.

'That little tramp had it coming, always hanging around switching her tail under our noses like an alley cat.'

'And you took advantage of a young girl who was desperate for someone to love her. She was reaching for a lifeline and got a selfish bastard instead,' I say. 'You kept her quiet for a while because you knew what she'd done to Louise. When her pregnancy was about to show she had it out with you by the flatbed. In another day or so she'd have been shouting it from the rooftop, so you lured her down to the river and choked the life out of her.'

208

'Well, you got me there,' he says. 'I sure screwed up my master plan.'

Galadette begins handling the rifle in a reckless manner, as if he'd like to pop someone but can't decide who should be first. Not having reached Louise before we did has reduced his options. Thad puts himself between Louise and the gun and Joe pushes Cookie behind him out of the line of fire.

'Listen Grady,' I say. 'Why don't we go on down to the station after I'm through here and I'll listen to your side of the story. Right now we've got to get medical care for Louise.' As I talk I'm moving my hand toward the gun in my holster, sidling away from the group, knowing things are about to go sideways.

Galadette spins toward me and raises the rifle. Cookie screams. I clear the holster and aim for center mass, pull the trigger and hear an ominous click as the pistol dry-fires. I'd be dead if Galadette hadn't paused for a self-satisfied smirk. His 'gotcha moment' was cut short by an ear-shattering blast. He's blown ten feet out of his shoes and lands face down on the ground. Walter Crowley steps into the clearing with a smoking shotgun in his hand.

I knew I had a guardian angel, but I didn't know he'd appear in the form of one hundred and ten pounds of hard jerky in patched overalls. My bad leg is trembling but Walter is as steady as an oak stump. What was it Hazel had said that night in Sparkey's? 'You do the next thing that needs to be done.' Well, Walter just did it.

I look at Crowley. 'Never underestimate a quiet man with a big gun,' I say.

'If I ever bagged anything bigger than a wild turkey,' he says, 'I thought it would be a deer.' He leans the gun against a tree and walks over to where his daughter is lying on the ground.

'I hear a siren,' says Joe.

'That's probably an ambulance. You want to help me move the cars so they can get in here?' I say.

'Sure can.' He gives me a quizzical look. 'Who are you?' he asks.

'The new guy.'

Louise is transported to Santa Paulina General with Thad at her side. Grady Galadette is off to the morgue and after questioning, Walter Crowley returns home to his little boys with his dog and his great-grandmother's basket.

Back at the station I bring Chief Garvey up to speed and tell Jim that tossing my gun off the bridge may not have been the best idea since Teague's piece nearly got me killed. After he's through laughing his ass off, I'm given a standard-issue service revolver and a shield that officially makes me one of the boys, a dubious distinction at best.

Before I leave the station I call the hospital. Thad says Louise will recover but she'll be there for a week under treatment for her wounds, exposure, dehydration and a lumbar sprain.

I eat a delicious turkey dinner that Jake left on a rolling cart outside my door at The Rexford. Never has a meal tasted this good. I wrestle my damp boots off swollen red feet and take a long, hot shower, before I collapse in bed. I'm asleep before I hit the pillow, a shot of brandy untouched on the nightstand and an unlit cigarette between my fingers.

★ ★ ★

Cookie and Joe drive out to his big house on the edge of town, where his cat waits in the window and an uncooked turkey sits in the refrigerator in a roasting pan.

'If we put it in the oven now, it should be done by morning,' says Cookie.

'I know,' says Joe, 'but what are we going to do in the meantime?'

Cookie smiles and touches his cheek.

'Oh Joe, I don't think we need a crystal ball to figure that out.'

12

A Daring Rescue

Hank patches through a long distance call at 9:00 a.m.

'Officer Dunning, my name is Marcella Estrada. I'm a waitress at the restaurant in Union Station down in L.A.' Now I'm wide awake. I jump out of bed and grab a pencil and paper. 'I saw the missing persons poster in the waiting room and I remember the girl in the photo. She got off the train early Sunday morning . . . petite blonde . . . black eye . . . torn blue raincoat. Not an image one soon forgets.'

'Yes, Miss Estrada, please go on.'

'As she was having coffee in the restaurant her purse was snatched off the table by an orange-haired man. An affluent-looking gentleman who'd been sitting at the counter gave chase, but the thief got away. He bought the young lady breakfast and they left together in his black Bentley. I wouldn't have been unduly concerned, except it's the third time I've witnessed this scenario with the same cast of characters and a different young lady. Each time the girl is young, pretty and in distress.'

'A set-up.'

'Exactly. I wish I'd said something at the time.' I wish she had too. 'He left me a business card a few months back when he forgot his wallet — you know, insurance on his breakfast tab. He came back a few days later and paid up.'

'Do you remember his name?'

'Officer Dunning, I'm looking at the card as we speak. Name: Ricardo Escobar. Two phone numbers. No business name.' I grab a pen and write them down as she reads them off. She gives me her number in case I need to get back in touch.

'Please, describe him as best you can.'

'My mother told me the devil is dangerous, not because he's evil-looking, but because he's the most gorgeous creature you'll ever lay eyes on. Get the picture, Officer Dunning?'

I dial the first number.

'El Toro.' A woman's voice. Husky. Drugged.

'Yes, ma'am, could you give me the El Toro address again? I'm from out of town and . . . '

Bed springs squeak and she hangs up. The second number is no longer in service. I have a check in my wallet from the Department. Hank cashes it for me. I tell him I have business in L.A., and I'll get it sewn up as soon as I can. I throw an overnight bag in the Caddy and spend the day speeding south through endless stretches of dreary emptiness and one-horse towns that comprise the Central Valley. I hit the outskirts of Los Angeles a couple hours after dark. I pull into a gas station on Santa Monica Blvd., near the intersection of Vine, and buy a local map. I call Marcella from the phone booth out front.

'Marcella, it's Jack Dunning,' I say when she answers. 'I made it down. Now I'm lost.'

'Don't worry about it, so is everyone

215

else in L.A. Listen, I've been talking to my husband Simon about your dilemma. He'd like to speak with you. Here, I'm putting him on.'

'Hello, Jack, I'm a broker with Star Realty. When Marcella told me who you were looking for, I went to my reverse directory. I tried to call you at The Rexford, but you'd already left. There are several property owners by the name of Escobar and several with the first name of Ricardo, most of them on the east side, but if your guy drives a Bentley he's probably the one at 2667 Eagle Crest in the Hollywood Hills.'

'Simon, thanks for going to the trouble. I really appreciate it.'

'Where are you now?' I tell him. 'You're ten, maybe fifteen minutes from his house even if you get turned around a couple times on the way.' I squint at my map.

'Thank you, sir. I see it.'

★   ★   ★

Friday evening at Eagle Crest, and the atmosphere is charged with anxieties and expectations. Horvat's party will include a Saudi diplomat and his three wives. That's a big deal, even for Hollywood. Rosalita has roasted a large tray of Cornish game hens stuffed with wild rice. They look juicy and golden brown, but she's so nervous that Angel has trouble getting her to settle down. There are side dishes of artichokes, Brussels sprouts with cheese sauce and a baked Alaska planned for dessert. Angel and Rosalita work together setting the table with flowers, candles, sparkling china, silver and crystal.

'Are you all right?' asks Angel. 'You don't seem yourself tonight.'

'Not really. I'm not used to waiting on such important people.'

'You'll do fine. I'll help you clean up after dinner. Then we'll sneak a bottle of orange liqueur to my room. How does that sound?'

'I'm so nervous.'

'I am too. Break a dish and get it over. That'll relieve some of the tension.'

They share a laugh. 'There, that's better.' Angel gives her a reassuring hug.

Rosalita looks beautiful in a turquoise dress and silver jewelry. Angel wears a cream-colored silk suit with a pearl necklace, her hair upswept in blonde swirls.

Bobo Horvat pulls into the driveway, followed by two limousines. Fritz parks the Caddy off to the side so the Prince's entourage can pull in front of the entrance. The Prince emerges from the first car. He's a short, pudgy man in immaculate white robes. His wives, concealed in black garments from head to toe, get out of the second car. The chauffeurs remain behind as everyone else is swept through the main entrance. Fritz, under strict orders, chains and locks the gate.

There are introductions all around, except for the wives, who remain silent and anonymous. Angel wonders how they manage to breathe in those suffocating veils. Once everyone is comfortably settled in the living room, Rosalita passes platters of hors d'oeuvres, pours drinks for those who want them and returns to the kitchen. So far so good.

One look at Horvat and Angel doesn't want anything to do with him professionally or otherwise. He's certainly not who he pretends to be. He senses her revulsion, but that doesn't stop him from crowding her on the couch until she's pressed uncomfortably against the arm-rest. He can't wait to offer her the job that doesn't exist but she won't discuss it.

'I'll call you on Monday,' she says. 'I'll get your number from Mr. Escobar.' She gives Escobar an imploring look. It isn't until he gives Horvat a hard-edged stare, that he backs off and gets up to pour himself another drink.

Escobar looks like a Latin movie star in his white suit and open-necked red silk shirt. His manners are impeccable, his friendly demeanor putting everyone at ease. It's only when he thinks no one is watching that Angel sees the tension in the set of his jaw. Beneath the smiles and joviality, she senses that something else is going on, but she doesn't know what.

Rosalita calls them to dinner. The Prince whispers something in Horvat's ear, something about the table and how it's set. Horvat turns to Escobar. 'The Prince's wives do not eat with the men,' he says. 'They can eat in the kitchen with Rosalita, or at the table when the men are through.'

Angel removes three of the place settings and helps the women get settled in the kitchen. She'd rather stay and distance herself from Horvat, but Escobar expects her to make a favorable impression on his guests.

When she re-enters the room everyone stops talking. The Prince nods and looks at her approvingly. The smug look on Horvat's' face puts her on edge. The men grin, raise their glasses and click rims in a comradely gesture. There's a hidden agenda beneath the smiles and polite conversation. Rosalita feels it too. Dinner seems interminably long, but the plates are finally removed and it's time for dessert. Fifteen minutes pass. No sounds of scurrying or click of dishware come from the kitchen.

'Angel, would you please see what's holding things up?' says Escobar.

She excuses herself and goes to the

kitchen. The entire baked Alaska is being energetically devoured by the Arab women.

'Where's Rosalita?' she asks, looking around. No one answers because they don't understand her. The kitchen door leading to the garden is ajar. An engine revs outside. Escobar rushes into the kitchen. The women scream and cover their faces.

'What the hell's going on?'

'I don't know,' says Angel.

Escobar runs through the house and throws open the front door as the Chevy roars toward the closed gate. Fritz, with Rosalita beside him, blasts through the gate with a terrible screech of metal. Angel watches as the gates become airborne and land in the street. Fritz drives over the twisted sections and barrels down the hill.

Rick turns on Angel in a fury and slaps her hard on the side of the head. She stumbles sideways, her ears ringing. He grabs her by the hair and shakes her, slapping her in the face with his free hand, while the Prince rushes around shouting orders in Arabic. His wives, once again heavily veiled, emerge from the kitchen.

'You set this up!' Escobar shouts at her. She's too stunned to reply and he's too enraged to care what she might say. The Prince and his wives pass them in a flap of long robes. He shouts something in Arabic to the chauffeur, who hustles the women into limo number two.

'Quickly, bring the girl,' says the Prince, grabbing Escobar's shoulder.

'Grab her!' screams Horvat. 'Let's get this done.'

The Prince holds the back door of his limo open. His driver stands ready with a pillow case and a length of rope. Before Angel has time to react, Horvat grabs one arm, Escobar grabs the other and they lift her off her feet. Horvat slaps a hand over her mouth to muffle her screams.

★ ★ ★

Rosalita clings to Fritz's arm. 'I can't believe we did it. You could have unlocked the gate. You have the key, don't you?'

Fritz holds up the key and tosses it out the car window.

'You can't imagine how long I've wanted to crash those gates. They represent everything I hate about that place.'

'Angel is alone now. Señor Escobar will be so angry.'

'First things first, Rosalita. We can only manage one thing at a time.'

They cruise through South-Central and park in the alley behind the pink house.

'Be very quiet,' he says, as they get out of the car. 'The neighbor has a scorched earth policy when it comes to trespassers. We'll go to the door and make our case. We can always call the police as a last resort.'

They walk to the front of the house and Rosalita rings the doorbell. Fritz stands a few feet behind her. An elderly woman opens the door in her robe, her gray hair in curlers, a baby bottle in her hand. From the look on her face they can tell she is expecting someone else.

'Yes?' she says, squinting over her bifocals. 'Do I know you?'

'My name is Rosalita Márquez. I am the mother of the little boy you take care of.'

'You must be confused. The baby's mother died of a drug overdose and his father is in prison.'

'That is not true, Señora. My husband was murdered and our baby stolen.'

An elderly man with a pipe appears in the doorway.

'If that tale is true, the police would be all over this place,' says the woman.

'I cannot call them. I am here illegally. It would get very complicated.'

'Please,' says Fritz, 'just give us a moment of your time to explain.'

'Let them in. I'd like to hear what they have to say,' says the man with the pipe. 'I'm George Tredwell. This is my wife Doris.'

'Pleased to meet you, sir. I'm Fritz Greenwold, a family friend.'

Once everyone is seated, Rosalita tells her story and explains the role Dutch Hackett played in the murder and abduction.

'Marjorie,' calls Mr. Tredwell. 'Bring

the baby. His bottle is ready.' The blonde woman appears with Matías in her arms. Rosalita stands. The baby looks at her. A few seconds pass in silence as the little boy rubs sleep from his eyes.

'Matías,' she says, softly. 'Niño.'

The baby gives an excited shriek. His arms fly out toward his mother and Marjorie can barely contain him.

'Mumumumum,' he says, and he is suddenly in Rosalita's arms, her tears falling into his hair.

The front door flies open, the doorknob punching a hole in the wall behind it. Everyone jolts. Matías howls and buries his head in his mother's shoulder. Dutch Hackett stands in front of them with a gun in his hand.

'Give me the baby,' he says, 'or I'll put a bullet in his head.' He looks at Fritz. 'I knew you wouldn't be able to stop snooping, but Escobar wouldn't listen to reason.' Fritz moves in front of Rosalita. 'You should thank me. The baby is going to a couple who can give him the best. He stays with this Mexican *puta*, he'll grow up to be one more dirt-poor peasant.'

'Hey you, carrot-head,' comes a deep voice from the porch behind Dutch. He turns toward the sound, fumbles his gun, almost drops it. A small dog flies screeching and snapping into the room, grabs the cuff of his trousers and whips it savagely like he's throttling a rat. Dutch shakes his foot and hollers curses but the creature sticks like a burr.

A tall black man stands in the light that spills through the doorway. Without uttering another word he flashes a mouthful of gold teeth and pumps three bullets into Dutch Hackett's stomach.

Dutch clutches his midsection and crumples to the floor like a bulky coat slipping from its hanger. Everyone in the room sits in shocked silence as the black man bends over and unhooks his dog from the pants cuff.

After the smoke settles and the witnesses recover from the initial shock, Mr. Tredwell walks across the room, steps over Hackett and touches the giant's arm.

'This can be a pretty unruly neighborhood,' says Mr. Tredwell. 'I'd like to introduce my neighbor, Ringer Jones, and PeeWee. They watch out for us old folks on the block.'

★ ★ ★

I get turned around a few times in the hills above Beachwood Drive. It would be helpful if some of the missing street signs had been replaced so I'd know if I was on a road or a bridle trail. It's a balmy night with soft Santa Ana winds whispering through the attics of the trees. A whirlwind of leaves floats over the hood of the car.

I find Eagle Crest and swing a left, step on the gas and feel the Caddy surge upward. I pull to the far shoulder of the road as a Chevy with front end damage zigzags down the hill like a runaway toboggan. I'm about to pull back onto the road when a black limousine with curtained windows flies past. By now my cop antennae are zinging. Something is going on up Eagle Crest. I proceed in a heightened state of awareness.

There are no streetlights and no curbs

to paint numbers on, only the illumination of a pale winter moon. What catches my eye is a pair of tall, scrolled gates lying in shambles at the side of the road. I pull over and let the car idle, then grab a flashlight from the glove box and shine it on the mailbox adjacent to the pillars that once supported the gates. 2667 Eagle Crest. I unconsciously touch the service revolver in my shoulder holster.

A second limousine is parked in front of a big yellow house at the end of a circular driveway. Its headlights are on and the engine idling as if it's just arrived or is about to leave.

A heated dispute is in progress between an enormous fat man, a gentleman in a white suit, a Middle-Easterner in native attire and a chauffeur who looks like he doubles as a bodyguard.

If Angel is here, I don't see her.

I turn off my headlights and roll down the window. The men are fighting about money, a great deal of money. The Arab says he's paid enough already. The fat man says he wants what they agreed on. The man in the white suit is telling them to calm down before the neighbors call the police.

I pull out my binoculars for a better look and focus on the man in the white suit. He's tall and slender with elegant carriage and an aristocratic air. If he were more beautiful he'd be a woman. It's Ricardo Escobar, handsome as the devil himself, just like Marcella said.

Until I find out what's going on and where Angel fits in, no one is going anywhere in a limo or anything else. I inch the Caddy crosswise between the brick pillars and turn off the engine. I take a deep breath and start walking up the driveway.

'Who are you?' says Fatso. 'Where the hell do you think you're going?'

'You're disrupting the neighborhood. People are trying to sleep.'

'What are you, the sandman making early rounds?'

'Just a concerned citizen.'

'I'm leaving,' says the Arab. 'Please, move your car.' I hear scuffling sounds from inside the limo. I get a bad feeling in the pit of my stomach.

'Like hell you're leaving,' says Fatso. 'You're not going anywhere until I get my money.'

'Let it go, Horvat,' says Escobar. 'You're making too much of this.'

'Now you're on their side?' he screams. Horvat mops his brow with a handkerchief already limp with sweat. 'You let him get away with this, you got no iron in your pitzel.'

'Please move your car,' says the bodyguard. 'The Prince's private plane is waiting.'

The Prince? This is getting interesting. I've listened to enough bickering. I reach in my pocket and flip my shield, then return it before someone gets too analytical. It's the real McCoy. It's just no good on L.A. turf.

'What's in the limo?' I say.

'None of your business,' says Horvat. 'You got no warrant.'

As the Prince walks around the front of the limo to get into the passenger side, Horvat whips out a gun and puts a bullet through the folds of his flowing robe. I pull my gun but before I can decide who to shoot, the bodyguard pulls a dagger from his sash. It sings through the air and plunges with a solid *whump* into Horvat's shoulder. If the Arab drives as well as he throws a knife, he'll cut through L.A. traffic like a pro.

Horvat falls to the ground shrieking. He curls into himself like a giant slug. I pick his gun out of the gravel and put it in my pocket.

'Everybody settle down. Are you all right?' I ask the Prince.

'Of course. Only Allah decides my fate.'

'That must be a comforting thought,' I say, but he misses the sarcasm.

'Hamed was protecting me. If he wanted the fat man dead, he would be dead.'

'I believe you. Now open up the limo.'

'It can't be done,' says the bodyguard. 'It is only a pet dog scratching to get out.'

'Then let him out.'

I hear sirens in the distance.

'Let him open it,' says the Prince. 'We're already behind schedule.'

'But . . . '

'Now, Hamed. Too much is being made

of a trivial matter.'

Escobar, who's managed to stay out of the fray, looks shell-shocked. Everything has slipped beyond his control. Pretty soon cops will be all over his private sanctuary. If his lawyer were here he'd know what spin to put on the situation. Feinstein would tell him to keep his mouth shut, and that's exactly what he intends to do.

My heart picks up an extra beat or two as I open the back of the limo. A girl lies bound on the floor with a pillow case over her head. I holster my gun, untie the rope around her neck and remove the pillow case. A cascade of blonde hair tumbles over the girl's slender shoulders. Broken pearls from her necklace are scattered on the carpet.

Angel Doll.

I remove the gag and untie her hands. She wraps her arms around my neck and I hold her, just hold her tight. I gather her into my arms and lift her out of the limo. A silent tear drops on my hand and I feel her warm breath on my cheek. The feeling that surges through me is what a weary traveler feels at the end of a long hard journey.

'Would anyone care to provide an explanation?' I look at the faces around me. 'What, no volunteers?'

'The Prince has diplomatic immunity,' says the bodyguard.

'I want to go home, Jack,' says Angel.

'That's why I'm here, baby. That's why I'm here.'

Three L.A.P.D. patrol cars pull up behind my Caddy and six officers jump out with guns drawn. I introduce myself, show them my badge and tell them why I'm here. I hand them Horvat's gun and tell them what I know. I'm glad it's their mess to untangle and not mine.

'Anybody know a Fritz Greenwald?' says the Sarge. 'He called to say a girl is being held here against her will. I could hear a baby laughing in the background.'

* * *

Angel and I are smoking at the window, looking down on Cork Street through the cold December rain. The room is warm and dark and neon from the theater dances in the flooded street.

Escobar and Horvat have lawyered up. There's so much evidence of criminal activity that they'll probably cop a plea to avoid a trial. The Prince, armed with immunity, flew back home with his three wives in tow. We receive a postcard from Mexico. Fritz, Rosalita and Matías remain in rural Sonora with her extended family.

If the Kapps return, they will find another family living in the tent and their daughter buried in an unmarked grave at the back of the cemetery. Someone who's a lot more forgiving than I would be, left flowers on her grave.

Mrs. Galadette returned to Oklahoma with a family who'd given up on California. She now resides with her spinster sister in Tulsa. Louise has recovered from her ordeal. She and Thad, with the blessing of Mr. Crowley, were married in the Baptist Church and are living in the flatbed house. Hazel stopped coming home and shares an apartment above the roadhouse with Sparkey. Mr.

Crowley, his little boys and Danny bravely soldier on by themselves.

Tonight Angel and I are going to The Fire Pit to hear Jake blow his sax. Hank is coming with us. Joe and Cookie will be there, as well as Jim, the Chief and some of the fellows from the Department. Swack has resigned under pressure and Green is on probationary status. I'm being kept on as a consultant.

Although I distrust the concept of happiness for its random and transitory nature, tonight I'm a happy man — happier than a guy with a drinking problem and a bum leg has a right to be.

The years that separate Angel and I are greater than the number of years she's resided on the planet. She's too young to grasp the implications of one day being a pretty woman in her prime stuck with an over-the-hill cop, and I'm too much in love to lend it credence.

Angel leans against my side all soft and warm like the night we danced at The Blue Rose. Tonight she wears the same silk dress with the pearl buttons. I remember how she undid those buttons, how the dress slid to the floor, how she led me to the bed and took me into her life.

'It's almost time to go,' she says, putting on that little dab of rose perfume.

'I know.'

'I'm a little nervous about meeting all those people, Jack.'

'Don't be. They'll love you just like I do.'

THE END

We do hope that you have enjoyed reading this large print book.

Did you know that all of our titles are available for purchase?

We publish a wide range of high quality large print books including:
Romances, Mysteries, Classics
General Fiction
Non Fiction and Westerns

Special interest titles available in large print are:
The Little Oxford Dictionary
Music Book, Song Book
Hymn Book, Service Book

Also available from us courtesy of Oxford University Press:
Young Readers' Dictionary
(large print edition)
Young Readers' Thesaurus
(large print edition)

For further information or a free brochure, please contact us at:
Ulverscroft Large Print Books Ltd.,
The Green, Bradgate Road, Anstey,
Leicester, LE7 7FU, England.
Tel: (00 44) **0116 236 4325**
Fax: (00 44) **0116 234 0205**

BAD THINGS HAPPEN
AT NIGHT

David Whitehead

The shadowy organisation known as the Council of Thirteen has only one goal: to bring the full terror of Hell to Earth. But there is one thing stopping them — Archer, a young man who has been raised from birth to fight the Council and its minions every step of the way. Archer is given orders to hunt down and slay a mysterious killer who is terrorising Paris. Along the way, he learns a secret that his masters have been keeping from him . . .

GRIM DEATH

Gerald Verner

Rich Mrs. Mallaby is hated by almost everyone in the village of Long Manton. When she is murdered in the church, Superintendent Hockley is faced with a big problem — nearly everybody has a motive. And what about the five hundred pounds which the dead woman had drawn out of her account? It looks like blackmail — but is it? Best-selling author Peter Hunt lives in the village, and is determined to solve the problem . . .

TEACH YOURSELF
TREACHERY

John Burke

Rachel Petersen's husband had drowned in Holland — so who is the man who appears at her house and claims to be that husband, substantiating his claim with a passport and detailed recollections of their brief married life? From the moment the stranger calling himself Erik Flemming Petersen steps through the door, there is no peace for Rachel. She determines to unravel the tangled threads of the mystery — only to find they are more tightly woven than she could have suspected . . .

PIT AND THE PENDULUM

John Gregory Betancourt

Peter 'Pit Bull' Keller is a ruined man ... A *wunderkind* at a Wall Street investment bank, his constantly racing mind started his downfall — a nervous breakdown, caused by working twenty-hour days, seven days a week. Then, just as he was beginning to pull himself together mentally, a taxi ran a red light and hit him, crippling him permanently. But despite his dependence on alcohol and painkillers, Peter's exceptional intelligence remain intact — as many criminals find to their cost ...

THE RETURN OF SHERLOCK HOLMES

Ernest Dudley

Though Professor Moriarty has perished at the Reichenbach Falls, Sherlock Holmes must still pit his wits against his old and deadly enemies — the malevolent blackmailer Charles Augustus Milverton, and the murderous Colonel Sebastian Moran . . . In this collection the author also gives us another of his own fictional creations: the sardonic Martin Brett — a more modern equivalent of the great detective — in four further ingenious stories of murder and mystery.